TANGO & LACE

MISTY DIETZ

OTHER TITLES BY MISTY DIETZ

Flirting with Fire (Colorado Heartthrobs Book 1)

Come Hell or High Desire

Unholy Proposal (Unholy Inc Book 1)

Unholy Legacy (Unholy Inc Book 2)

———

Don't wanna miss any new titles?

Sign up for Misty's newsletter and receive a free book!

MISTY MEDIA
September 2016
eBook ISBN: 978-1-943716-04-3
Print ISBN: 978-1-943716-05-0

Edited by: Pam Dougherty, www.TheWriteActor.com

ONE

"Turn it up, Natalia!" Mya Castillo pushed out of the wicker chair, her hips and shoulders already rolling to the Reggaeton beat dropping from the wireless speaker perched on their elderly neighbor's backyard bar.

Mya's sister, Natalia, grinned and set down the latest copy of *TeenVOGUE* as she uncurled from her chair in the shade. "Yeah, let's wake all the neighbors."

Mya gently pulled seventy-eight-year-old Rosie Strickland to her feet. "I love this song. Dance with me, *chula*."

The Colorado morning sunshine struck Rosie's shoulder-length, pewter hair. "I'll take my broom after old man Peters if he growls about the noise."

Mya laughed, her heart lighter than it had been in weeks. After Rosie's heart attack last month, they weren't sure she'd survive. Mya had been in Rosie's garden when Rosie had collapsed in the dirt. *Can't lose another one I love.*

Mya and Nat's older brother, Cole eased toward the edge of Rosie's leaky roof where he and two other men had been sweating under the July sun for three hours already. "I doubt Rosie's doctor prescribed exertion in heat like this. Get her in the shade, Mya. You know better," he scolded.

Rosie smiled up at Cole, the healthy pink on her Navaho cheekbones a welcome sign after her pallor the last couple of weeks. "The heat and movement feel good, honey." She took seventeen-year-old Nat's hand, forming a circle of three with Mya. "I'll petrify if I sit in my recliner another hour."

Mya winked at Cole. "Get back to work, *hermano*. We're busy." He shook his head, turning back to the other shirtless men ripping the last of the shingles off the roof. When the song ended, Mya returned Rosie to her chair and raised the table umbrella. She was walking toward the bar to refill her lemonade when someone started yelling.

Mya swung around, her gaze flying upward. Arturo Gutierrez was head-first on his belly, slipping down the uppermost pitch of Rosie's roof, gravity quickly pulling him toward the leaf gutter which couldn't possibly hold his weight. "Cole, *mira*! Artie's falling!" she screamed, pointing and running toward the edge of the patio where Arturo would drop in seconds.

Cole scrambled sideways in a crouch down the roof, then went to his knees, grabbing Arturo by his pant leg and countering backwards to stop his descent. When they both started sliding, Ty Beckinsale, one of Rosie's grandsons, grabbed Cole around the waist and went to his ass on the roof.

"Nat, grab Rosie's stack of blankets inside by the rocking chair!" Mya barked, scrambling to collect all the outdoor cushions. Cole's grunts mingled with Ty's world record number of 'fucks' delivered in five seconds. Arturo's head appeared over the edge of gutter, his right cheek bloody. Nat flew out the back door, her arms full of blankets, and tossed them in a pile underneath the roof's edge. Mya tossed the last of the cushions on top of the blankets, then raised her arms to break Arturo's fall, her heart pounding in her chest. "If you break your neck or kill me in the process, I'll be seriously pissed off, *cabrón*."

Arturo's hand came over the edge—*shit!*—arms, shoulders—

And stopped.

He hung mid-air, half his chest on, half off, the roof. In the next instant, Cole and Ty hauled him back up, clipping his chin on the gutter on their last brute tug.

All the air evaporated from Mya's chest. She sank to her butt on the pillows and blankets piled on the flagstone patio. She'd *told* Artie he shouldn't be taking any chances right now. Roofing was dangerous, and with their Argentine Tango USA Championship coming up in three weeks, neither of them could afford to get sick, maimed, or killed. But of course, his big Cuban heart had insisted he help Cole and Ty with Miss Rosie's roof.

Mya closed her eyes and laid back on the cushions, listening to the men follow up their fears with machismo. Ty wasn't Cuban like Cole and Arturo, but being ex military and a grandson of Rosie's meant he had alpha male written in his DNA just as fiercely. Mya brought her arm across her eyes, letting her heart rate return to normal.

"You alright, Mya?" Rosie called.

As Mya lifted her arm in a thumbs-up, a shadow slid across her closed eyelids. Nat and Rosie gasped at the table behind her. Goosebumps skated over her skin as she shot up to a sitting position, her gaze feasting on six feet of hard-bodied, left-brained genius.

Damnation.

Jackson Whiteside.

What was HE doing here? He'd gone and messed her up something good when he'd left two years ago on a prestigious international grant to unearth more Dead Sea Scrolls in Israel's West Bank. He looked even more *wow* today than he had when she'd slammed the door in his face after he'd shared his achievement. His mahogany hair looked thicker, standing up with artless masculinity, reminding her how much she used to love running her fingernails across his scalp. How he'd groan and nuzzle into her breasts like a wild beast tamed by her touch. The perfectly criminal lips, the ever-present five o'clock shadow, the bronzed skin, and *those eyes*.

Those damned steel-blue eyes behind those brainy tortoiseshell glasses. *Balls.*

"Hello, Mya."

Oh my god, and that voice.

Her eyes closed on a slow blink as her gray matter swooned. Nat and Rosie swarmed around him—touching him as though to reassure themselves their Ivy League idol had actually returned. *Sick.* Mya pushed up to her feet, ignoring his outstretched hand.

"Ty finally guilted you enough to come back?" she asked, sounding even more bitchy than she'd planned. Nat glared at her. Well, too bad. He deserved a good rebuke. Rosie had needed help from her family long before her heart attack, but had he stepped up to answer repeated calls from his older cousin?

Hell, no.

At least until now.

Mya's stomach fluttered, her skin hot and prickly. Rosie grabbed hold of Mya and Jackson's wrists and brought each of their hands to her bosom, tears welling in her eyes. When their skin connected, Mya felt the heat of Jack's hand down to the tips of her bare toes.

Don't look at him. Don't. You. Dare. His potent stare could trap her soul and not let go until he'd wrung her out and left her panting on the wall of his chest.

But of course, she looked at him.

Her lips parted with the pain of memory. Then he blinked, and his *I-remember-everything* look was gone. She pulled her hand from Rosie's grasp and turned to walk unsteadily back to the bar, this time adding a shot or three to her lemonade. The guys on the roof had made it safely down and were greeting the geoarchaeologist extraordinaire.

Mya leaned her butt against the bar, drinking half the lemonade in one swallow. She knew he'd eventually come home. Ty mentioned that he and Rosie's four other grandsons were working out a schedule so each of them would come to Fort Collins to help look after Rosie and give some TLC to her wonderful, but neglected stone house. She'd been dying to ask Ty when Jack's turn was, but couldn't bring herself to do it. Funny Rosie hadn't mentioned anything...

She narrowed her eyes at the sweet old lady.

Rosie looked up as though sensing Mya's gaze—*aaa*nd she freaking winked. She'd *known* Jackson was on his way home, but the little shit hadn't said a word. Heat flooded Mya's face. She opened her mouth to give Rosie a piece of her mind about how this—

"Mya, would you mind running over to your place to grab the slow cooker you borrowed last week? I'm going to make a roast. Let's have a party tonight!" Rosie clapped her hands with keen eyes, looking ten years younger and twenty times tougher than she had fifteen minutes ago.

"Sure, let me get right on that! Nothing like welcoming the prodigal grandson home," Mya lobbed the words like a grenade, but everyone was so enamored with the rock-star scientist, they didn't hear. Or they didn't care. *Idiots with short memories.*

Well, not her. She remembered *everything*—whether she wanted to or not.

She swiveled from the sappy reunion, but before she could cross the lawn between her and Rosie's yards, a hand touched her elbow. She shook off the grip and swung around. "No touching!"

One side of Arturo's lips raised, his chocolate brown eyes understanding and...sad. "If that's the case, you might as well start looking for a new dance partner right away."

"Sorry, Artie. I thought..." Her voice trailed off, but she didn't need to finish. Arturo already knew all about her and Jack's messy ending. Unfortunately, he'd been a pawn in her bid to keep Jackson stateside.

Yeah, damn.

That was the part she always wanted to forget. It was so much easier being angry with Jackson for leaving. But the older she got and the more time passed, the harder it was to excuse her callous treatment of both men while in the depths of her heartache. Artie had forgiven her, but she didn't deserve it.

She had no idea how Jack felt. This was the first time she'd communicated with him since he'd left.

"Sorry," she repeated, reaching up to pick a dandelion seed off his blood-encrusted cheek. He still hadn't put his shirt on because of his shingle road-rash. "Come with me, let's get you cleaned up."

He stopped her with a hand on her shoulder. "I'll get

the slow cooker and take care of myself. You stay here and get things squared away."

He really was a prize. Kind, sexy, hard-working, and committed to family. She was obviously flawed not to fall in love with him. She glanced where Jack stood with the others. He was frowning at her. She frowned right back and stormed across his gramma's yard to her own. "*Andale*, Arturo!"

Artie ran to catch up. "If you walk away, you're going to look weak to him."

"Rosie gave me an order," she huffed.

"*Right*. Since when do *you* follow anyone's orders? Come on, you need to deal with this now. If you don't, your concentration on the dance floor will suffer, and then we'll lose the competition. You know damn well I'm right."

She stopped. He was. If her thoughts were preoccupied with Jackson, there was no way they'd perform well enough to place in the competition's top three. A local sports retailer had offered to sponsor her very own dance studio *if* they placed. Aspire Athletic would not only give her the money, but also the credibility she needed to establish herself in an already-crowded dance-instruction marketplace.

She *had* to have a top-three placement at Nationals.

She pressed her palms to her temples. She was being selfish. Not only did Rosie need looking after for at least another month, her house needed numerous repairs. If Rosie's family was stepping up to the task, Mya could deal with her Jackson Whiteside hangups. Then maybe she'd be free to find love again.

"You're right." She kissed Arturo's intact cheek, hoping he could sense everything she couldn't put to words. How she was sorry they couldn't be more, how much she appreciated his friendship, how badly she wanted them to place at Nationals. She pulled back, ignoring the warmth in his eyes. "Thanks for the pep talk. The slow cooker is in the pantry on the second shelf. Gauze and antiseptic are in my bathroom. If you need stitches, I'll drive you to the clinic."

Her shoulders dropped as Artie walked to her back door. As good as they were together on the dance floor, she knew she danced better with Jackson. Dancing with Jack was like making love in public. All his massive brainpower focused on her body, his intensity all-consuming. A drug that left her high and needy.

Never again.

She inhaled, then exhaled heavily—twice—before turning around with the most devil-may-care smile she could muster.

Jack had been laughing at something obviously colorful Ty had said, but as soon as his eyes met hers, his smile melted away, and his gaze went shuttered.

Mya's heart went *lub-dub.* Cole's girlfriend, Ivy, had a mantra, *Never let'em see you sweat.*

Yeah.

Game on, professor.

TWO

A trickle of sweat slid down Jackson's spine, his tongue like sandpaper in his mouth. *Breathe.* It was only natural that seeing Mya after all this time would jack his blood levels of adrenaline and cortisol. A purely physiological reaction, and therefore, something that made sense. Hormonal response could be picked apart, compartmentalized, and ultimately ignored.

Still, though, he couldn't tear his gaze from those narrow, arching brows over her wide, hazel eyes with their thick black lashes. Smooth, caramel skin with the bewitching little mole one inch from the edge of her lips that were always parted in laughter or mockery. That fall of shiny black hair and compact, *flexible* body that his hands and mouth would remember until the day they put his bones in a box. Her tiny frame was still lean, but more lush somehow. His gaze swept across her breasts pressed snugly against the red, spaghetti-strap tank top.

Her breathing seemed to still. His heart hammered double-time in his chest.

Christ.

It's dopamine.

That's all that was happening right now. Another neurotransmitter hormone dumped into this biological miasma. How Mya's beauty could grow even more hypnotic since—and in spite of—the last time he'd seen her was damned irritating. Especially seeing her with Arturo again.

This science of love bullshit was why he'd driven hard into the geosciences instead of straight up archaeology. Archaeology delved into the impact of emotion on people's lives. Earth sciences, on the other hand, made no emotional demands on his work. And that was exactly how he liked it.

He turned to Rosie to give his neurotransmitters time to cool off. "Gramma, don't go to any trouble for me. I need to take my gear to the research lab at the university. I don't know how long it'll take, so don't worry about supper."

"Nonsense! It's not even noon. You can work for several hours before we eat." Her eyes twinkled. "I'm so happy you're home!"

He smiled and wrapped her in a hug, unfortunately turning in the direction where Mya stood with one of her infamous You're-Going-Down smiles. *Great.*

When he released Rosie, Mya crossed her arms in front of her, drawing his gaze back to her bewitching cleavage. "Why don't you take *tu abuela* with you to CSU while you get settled in? The doctor doesn't like her to be alone for long stretches of time yet."

It was a challenge if he'd ever heard one. He really couldn't blame her. She'd gone over and above to care for his gramma when he and his other family members had been out of state, or in his case, out of the country. Mya did nothing half-way, whether it was dancing, fighting, or fucking. It was what he'd loved best about her even as it simultaneously drove him crazy.

He resisted the urge to look at his watch, wishing those bluish-gray altostratus clouds hovering over the foothills would start dumping buckets of rain so there could be a natural, non-awkward end to this discussion. "I appreciate everything that you, Cole, and Nat have done for Rosie. It means a lot knowing she has neighbors like you who treat her more like family than a friend. I plan to keep close tabs on her, but I don't know what to expect this afternoon." He turned from Mya's raised eyebrow to Rosie. "I don't want you to get bored or tired, which I would imagine might be the case, at least for today. I promise, I'll bring you to work with me when I have the lay of the land."

"How convenient for you," Mya snapped.

"Don't start, *lobita*," Cole said, starting back up the ladder. Ty, Nat, and Rosie had also quietly dispersed, which was a bad sign. *Time to head out.* Organizing his tools in his new office would be a good way to decompress. Hopefully, they'd arrived from overseas.

"When someone wants to do something nice like host a welcome-home party for you, it's bad manners to reject their offer. I would've thought spending two years in the Holy Land would've amended your lack of social graces." Mya had drawn closer to him, one hand gathering her long hair into a fist like she always did when gearing up for a fight. Her eyes flashed, and a highly distracting flush had begun to spread across her chest. How far south did that flush ride across her satin skin?

Not your business anymore. Keep your damn distance.

Jack forced his lips to tip upwards. "I will not be influenced by immature attempts to provoke me. My gratitude for your nurturing nature stands, as does my position on bringing Rosie to the university. Being that I have yet to visit the department, however, it would be insensitive of me to bring her into a situation that I cannot predict. Now, good day, Mya."

Her apparent shock at his stiff formality bought him precious seconds. Gramma's back door was only five steps away. Five, unbearably long steps. Aaand...

He didn't make it before Mya lobed her next emotional hand grenade.

"You think you can just come back here and be the hero, but you have no idea how hard this has been on her. Or how run down her house has gotten!"

He swung back around, fully cognizant that his cerebral cortex was losing ground to his limbic system as Mya's emotional hand grenade exploded. His face, chest, and neck grew hot with feelings that had been ignored for a long time. He closed his eyes and reached for calm.

Ablation, accretion, active layer, alluvial fan, alpha decay...

He ran through more geological terminology, starting with the letter *A*, feeling his blood pressure begin to normalize. She'd somehow slashed and burned though his shelved emotions in less time than it took him to calibrate a gravimeter using short data sets. He ran both hands through his hair to release some energy. "I left Jordan as soon as I could without jeopardizing my team's entire project. I've accepted a position in CSU's Geoscience Department so I can take my turn to be near her and so *our* family can relieve the burden from *your* family. I also plan to review and repair any electrical work in her house. What else do you want from me, Mya?"

"First of all, Rosie's never been a burden. To suggest otherwise shows how out of touch you are. Secondly, from what I understand, your position at CSU is only temporary.

Not because *la universidad* doesn't want to keep you, but because you—like always—can't commit to anything."

Low blow. "You delusional little hellion. Do you really want to hash through this again?"

"Anyone for some lemonade?" Rosie called in a falsely bright voice.

Mya's angry gaze stayed pinned on his. "Rehashing is a waste of time. I have better things to do, *hombre*."

She was actually going to walk away *now*?

He grabbed her arm, but she shook him off. "No touching!"

"Fine!" He yelled, totally not recognizing himself, goddammit.

"Yes, fine! *Perfecto!*" she yelled back several decibels louder.

Neither one moved. From his peripheral vision, he noticed all activity had stopped on the roof and on the patio.

It had taken him two years to think he might actually be able to see her again without his heart breaking. Without thinking of all the what-might-have-beens.

And all of twenty minutes to show him how wrong he'd been to think he'd ever be able to look at her beautiful, passionate face and not remember how miserably it had all ended.

I can't do this with her. Not again.

He clenched his teeth, the hollow in his chest expanding unbearably until he finally forced his feet to pivot away just as a scream erupted from Mya's house.

THREE

"Natalia!" Heart pounding, Mya followed Jackson as he sprinted toward her house. She smacked into his backside when he stopped abruptly inside the back door and put his arms out so she couldn't pass. "Move! This is *my* house, and that's *my* sister!"

She heard loud gasps of pain, alternated with coughing and wheezing. When Jack crouched down, Mya saw Artie lying on his side on her kitchen floor, clutching his eyes, saliva and mucus coming from his mouth and nose, his body contorting in what looked like a tremendous effort to breathe. Nat stood just inside the patio door, exhibiting many of the same symptoms.

"Everyone back up, the house is contaminated!" Jack ordered, then held his breath as he grabbed Arturo under the armpits and dragged him outside.

Mya pulled Nat out into the yard and put her hands on her sister's back, crooning to her in English and Spanish as Nat bent over, coughing and spitting into the grass.

"Oh dear, what happened?" Rosie's face paled as she walked between the two yards.

Jack's lips compressed when he glanced at his grandmother. "I think he's been gassed," he said. "I saw this in Syria multiple times." Arturo coughed, gagged, and vomited, his eyes squeezed shut and watering like crazy. Jack turned to Cole. "Call 911. This was more than hand-held pepper spray. It must've been a tear gas canister like the police use for riot control. I didn't take time to look for the canister, but once the authorities get here they should be able to find it. Arturo must've taken a direct hit to the face. And with his chest and face injuries from the roofing incident, that gas might do more damage than usual."

Cole turned away to make the emergency call. Jack instructed Mya to put Nat under Rosie's shower for several minutes, fully clothed, using lots of soap.

"I'm not helpless, Jack. Mya, I'll take your sister. You see to Artie." Rosie reached for Natalia. "Come, darling."

While Rosie and Nat made their way inside, Jack hauled Mya's water hose over and bent down to Arturo. "We need rinse the chemicals from your eyes as soon as possible. I know it hurts like hell, but you have to try to keep them open, okay?"

Mya saw concern riding under Jack's focus. She spoke quietly to Artie, trying to keep him calm as Jack flushed so much water in Artie's face she thought he'd drown. Ty came around the side of the house with the first responding police officers in tow. Soon the paramedics arrived, the SWAT hazmat team shortly after that. Mya wanted to follow the ambulance to make sure Artie would be okay, but first she had to make sure Nat was alright. And the police had questions since it was her home.

What could she tell them? Her front door had been locked. Not her back door, but they'd been hanging out next door at Rosie's with a view of Mya's backyard. How had someone gotten in, and why? Artie said he hadn't seen his attacker, so he couldn't help.

Officer Ramos had tired eyes and the swarthy good looks of an aging movie star. "I'll get a report from the hazmat team after they've had a chance to go through everything in the house. Have you had problems with break-ins in the past?"

Mya shook her head. "Never. There was some minor vandalism down the street about a year ago, but this neighborhood is generally quiet," she replied. She felt Jackson's gray-blue eyes pinned on her. She glanced over at him. His polo and jeans clung to his perfect body, soaked through from power rinsing the toxin off Arturo.

He put his hands on his hips and frowned at her. "You have a feud with anyone?"

"You think this is my fault?"

"I'm not implying that. But if your job as a 911 dispatcher inadvertently landed some whack job in trouble, and they got angry enough to try to hurt you, we should be aware of that. We need to know if this is premeditated or random."

She didn't know. Wasn't that awful? She'd handled several dicey situations where drugs were involved and criminals ended up in the District Attorney's cross-hairs. If this violence had been intended for her, she didn't know how she'd ever be able to forgive herself for putting Artie in this position.

"Mya?"

She looked up. Jack's voice had softened. His eyes, too.

"I honestly don't know," she replied.

A man in a plastic hazmat suit came out of her house, heading for Officer Ramos. "The front door lock was picked and several drawers were upended in one of the bedrooms.

At first glance, it seems like a standard break-in with the perp being surprised by the victim's unexpected entrance. But I haven't seen one of these bad boys in a long while." The hazmat tech held up a metallic-silver canister with *RIOT CS SMOKE* in blue lettering.

"Seems pretty ballsy with all of us outside next door." Cole's gaze swung from Ramos to Mya. "Why don't you call Andre. He stayed overnight at his buddy Matt's, right?"

The blood froze in Mya's veins. "*Dios.*" She hadn't heard from their eighteen-year-old brother since last night around ten pm, and her mind seized on all sorts of horrible scenarios.

"Don't overreact, *lobita.*" Cole put an arm around her shoulders and squeezed. "He's fine, though he'll be pissed that you woke him up before noon. But he needs to know what's going on." He reached for the phone in her hands. "Here, maybe I should talk to him."

She smacked his hand away and placed the call to Andre, her heart-rate easing as soon as his crabby voice answered. When she hung up, the hazmat tech handed the tear gas canister to Ramos. "Ms. Castillo, you can't return to your property until you've had a specialty remediation service clean up all the residue. I'll leave a list of locally-based services we recommend."

"Doesn't tear gas evaporate rapidly?" Cole asked.

The hazmat tech nodded. "In open-air environments, yes. But the air conditioning was on in the house when the canister deployed, so the toxins were introduced into the HVAC system. If that's not addressed, long term exposure to the toxin can cause extreme blistering and inflammation of the skin and respiratory systems."

"It seems unlikely a run-of-the-mill thief would be carrying riot gas. This can't be random," Jack said. He had to be standing directly behind her. His body heat touched all along her back.

She closed her eyes like that would be enough armor against him. "Why? Because it makes more sense that someone could hate me this much?"

Jackson turned her toward him. "Jesus, Mya, no." He walked her away from the others until they stood under the boughs of the willow tree Cole had planted the afternoon they'd laid their father to rest. The concern in Jack's eyes and the memory of the last kiss they'd shared under the dappled shade of this special tree made her heart bump and skitter.

"Our relationship ended miserably, but I don't want us to be at each other's throat while I'm here. I want us to get along...and I want you to be safe. The thought of you in danger is untenable," he said.

Logic and unflinching honesty had always been hallmarks of Jack's character. She was grateful for his concern. And worried about the safety of her and Cole's two high school-aged siblings who still lived under her roof.

Cole approached the tree, looking at Jackson. "Andre, Nat, and Mya can stay with Ivy and me."

She pushed the branches aside to stand in front of him. "I'm right here, Cole. I'll make decisions for myself. Besides, you and Ivy don't have room for all three of us at your place."

His serious hazel gaze bored into hers. "Andre can take the sofa. You and Nat can share the queen in the guest room. It'll be tight, but we can make it work."

"She can stay at Rosie's," Jack interjected. Mya tried to keep the shock off her face as he continued, "Ty's heading back to Noble Pass to be with Faith, so I'll claim the guesthouse out back. Knox won't be here for another month, and Blake and Adam the two months after that, so the best guest room in the main house is open."

His gramma's property was the only one in the neighborhood that had two city lots, the back ends of which connected. Her home was situated next to Mya's, while the guesthouse sat on the lot behind the stone house. "Thanks for the offer, but—"

"That's perfect. I'm sure Mya will behave herself." Cole turned to her. "You can borrow some clothes and whatever else you need from Ivy until you're able to get some of your own cleaned."

Mya grabbed her hair in a makeshift ponytail instead of wrapping her fingers around her brother's or Jack's neck. "You two can't railroad me about where I park my ass for the next couple of days."

"Maybe not, but as a mature adult, *hermana*, I'm sure you're grateful for Jack's offer so everyone can be more comfortable."

Heat traveled up her neck in waves. Her mouth opened, ready to spew a semi-trailer load of creative Spanish insults, but she clamped it shut and glared instead. This was humiliating. Arguing with her brother in front of the professor about her level of maturity. Unreal. *Count to ten.* She'd look so much worse in front of Jack if she lost her temper.

She released her hair and squeezed her fists at her sides while she gave Cole one more scathing glance before turning back to Jack. "I appreciate your offer. I'll try not to inconvenience you and Rosie too much."

"I'm not concerned." He turned away, ending the conversation, then walked into Rosie's house where she *should* have gone minutes ago to check on Nat. Instead, she stood there like a moron, watching him as he made another phone call, not only trying to comprehend what she'd just agreed to, but also his nonchalant acceptance of her up in his personal space for the first time in two years.

They'd gone from habañero hot to cold turkey in moments. Fast forward twenty four months...and the hurt, confusion, and abandonment still felt like it was yesterday.

She could see Jack through Rosie's tall, wide kitchen windows where his fingers ran across the white cabinets in search of a water glass. She remembered those hands touching her with such confidence, such possession. She shivered in the rising heat of the day, the police and medics in and out of her own kitchen behind her. She watched Jack's hands as he filled the glass at the sink, imagining the strong sinew of his forearms, the corded muscles of his biceps, the rise of his shoulders, every line of his body, poetry.

He wasn't concerned about her in his space, huh?

Well, *she* was.

And she was damned if she was gonna be the only miserable *pendeja* in this arrangement. Sometimes offense was the best defense, especially because Jackson Whiteside always brought his A-game.

FOUR

Once he'd checked on Natalia, Jackson called his cousin Blake Strickland to make sure he got his ass down to Fort Collins to take his turn with gramma. When Blake answered on the first ring, Jack relaxed for the first time since laying eyes on Mya.

"Hey, Blake, how's life in the concrete jungle?"

"More comfortable than sweating it out in the Middle East digging up old scrolls written by men in white beards, I'm sure," the internet entrepreneur returned with a smile in his voice.

Jack laughed. "At least I don't sit on my ass staring at a computer screen all day, every day. You hear about gramma?"

"Yeah. How's she doing?"

"She'll bounce back. I just got to Fort Collins." *And I have no idea how I'll deal with my Cuban heartache for an entire month.* "Ty's been here for a while now."

"How's he feeling?"

"Real good. In fact, we'll finish reshingling her roof tomorrow, then he'll head back to Noble Pass since I'm here.

We need to take turns staying with gramma. Give her some company and fix up the house. The exterior looks like shit, and who knows what needs tinkering on the inside. If there's any electrical work to be done, I'll have that covered by the end of the month. She can't do it by herself."

"Okaaay," Blake said, drawing out the word.

"Time to man up, buddy. I'm here through July, and Knox said he'd come after football camp in August. That means you're on deck in September."

"What? I thought Mya looked after her."

Jack clenched his jaw. "I'm not discussing Mya."

"Touchy much?"

"Rosie's our blood, our responsibility. I'm calling so you have time to plan, Mister Big Wig. Can you make it?" Jack lifted the phone away from his ear with Blake's big sigh.

"Yeah, I'll make it."

"And leave your monkey suits at home. You'll need real work clothes. The place needs some TLC."

"Shit."

Jack chuckled. Blake was so easy to antagonize—especially when it concerned a cute graphic designer by the name of Charlotte. "Hang in there, big man. I'll see you later."

When Jack returned outside to join Cole and Ty, they were conferring with the police regarding anything that might be useful to track the perpetrator. Unfortunately, without any witnesses, the police couldn't provide any immediate answers.

Answers that could eliminate ambiguity.

He hated ambiguity. And restlessness.

And loose ends.

Why *the hell* had he suggested Mya stay at Rosie's? He knew she'd take the offer. She'd always made sacrifices for her family's comfort and well being, no matter the fallout to herself.

It was a trait that had both inspired and perplexed him many times over the years.

She was a woman of extremes. Being in her sphere was like finding out you'd won the lottery, and in the next breath, informed you had one week to live.

Mya lived life large and in blinding color. It was exhilarating and amazing and utterly exhausting.

He'd returned to Colorado to help fix up Rosie's house and keep an eye on her as she continued to heal. Her heart attack had been a wake-up call for him and the rest of his cousins. Rosie had always been a fixture in their lives—as strong and colorful as Mya.

Someone you thought would always be there.

Until they weren't

He'd also come back to Fort Collins to rest after two grueling years of international fieldwork.

And maybe to finally face the ghosts of the past that still haunted the dark hours of the night when he awoke, reaching for Mya.

He'd mentally prepared to see her with Arturo. The two had become dance partners shortly after he'd left for Israel. Gramma had been the devil, sending him pictures of the pair in their dance finery, accepting award after award. He'd poured over those pictures as penance for his part in their painful break up.

For her part, Mya had viewed his decision to accept the Dead Sea Scrolls assignment as another abandonment. When she was fifteen, her police officer father had been gunned down during a domestic dispute gone horribly wrong, and two years later, her mother's battle with ALS left her and Cole to not only fend for themselves, but also their two younger siblings.

Coming home to Fort Collins, he'd prepared himself to be happy for her and Arturo. Prepared to finally accept that they weren't meant for each other—regardless of how amazing he and Mya had made each other feel in the beginning, before her insecurities and his intolerance of her volatility got in the way. He'd hoped seeing Mya and Arturo together, happy, would finally let him move on.

Jackson was a man of science, not emotion, but this morning when he'd watched them together, even he could sense that their connection wasn't anything like what *he'd* shared with Mya. *Doesn't mean she doesn't love Arturo.*

Mya and Arturo had so much in common, and that counted for a lot. Passion could only sustain a marriage for so long. He was beginning to wonder if that's all he and Mya had ever had.

He handed his business card to Officer Ramos, asking him to call if they developed any leads, since Mya was going to be staying next door. He looked over at her, standing on Rosie's patio, drying off Nat's hair with one of his grandmother's out-dated pink bath towels. His chest squeezed when she glanced up. The layered emotion in her beautiful eyes made his walls rise another brick higher even as he wanted to yank her to him and feel her body ignite under his.

Mya Carmen Castillo was still his kryptonite.

Too bad he wasn't Superman, capable of leaping over five-foot-four inch Cuban-American sirens in a single bound.

Fuck.

Mya wrapped another towel around Nat's shoulders

and walked directly toward them. "Can I at least go inside to get my purse and keys?" she asked Ramos.

"Why?" "To go where?" Jack and Cole said at the same time.

A familiar furrow appeared between her arched brows. "Must you two bellow? Where do you *think* I'm going? Someone should go to the hospital to check on Artie."

Ramos shook his head. "Sorry, no one can enter the property until it's passed inspection. That means your vehicle, too."

Mya pursed her lips. "How long will that take?"

"Have you called any of the remediation services on the list yet?" When Mya shook her head, Ramos continued. "I'd call as soon as possible. Those guys stay busy. You'll want to get on their schedule."

Jackson ignored the shaft of jealousy over Mya's obvious frustration about not being able to get to Arturo. "I can drive you to the hospital."

She turned to Jack with a strangely blank look. "I'll take Cole's truck. In case you don't remember, I learned to drive when I was twelve."

An image of her sitting on a stack of pillows so she could see over the dashboard flashed through Jack's mind.

"I need my truck today, but I can drop you off," Cole said from the doorway.

Mya closed her eyes briefly as though praying for patience. "I don't want or need either of you to babysit or shuttle me hither and yon. You heard them say this appears to be a standard break in, right?"

"They don't know much about anything yet." Cole glanced over as Nat and Rosie approached them. "Let me call Ivy. She mentioned wanting to take you, Nat, and Andre to her parents' house in Denver for some R and R before school starts next month. Her parents have a huge house with a pool."

"I'm in!" Nat said, refolding a faded and frayed pink towel.

Cole took his phone out of his back pocket. "After I talk to Ivy, I'll call your 911 dispatch supervisor and explain what's going on, Mya, so don't worry about work."

Mya crossed her arms over her chest. "I'm *not* leaving town, Cole. I committed to coaching two middle school students who are competing in the National DanceSport Youth Championship. And I'm not leaving Artie."

"Fine. Then you'll stay with Jack and Rosie. But first, come get some things from Ivy until you have access to your stuff."

She opened her mouth like she was going to protest, but Rosie put her hand on Cole's forearm.

"Do you think Ivy would mind if I tagged along to Denver?" she asked, "It sounds fun, and I could really use a diversion." When she winked at Jack over her shoulder, his gut bottomed out.

"*No*," "*No way!*" he and Mya gasped simultaneously. If gramma went to Denver, that would leave him alone with Mya in a place that already bled too many memories.

Cole held up a hand to silence them, but before he could speak, his phone rang. While Cole answered the call, Jack turned to Rosie, his pulse on hyperdrive. "I came back to Colorado to be with you, gramma. Plus you should be near your doctors." *Or I'll have a heart attack myself.*

Mya nodded. "Yeah, Rosie, you need to keep things low key. We don't want you to have another episode. You should stay home."

Rosie smiled serenely at both of them. "Aww, you two

are sweet to fret, but Ivy's mother is a cardiothoracic surgeon, so I'll be in good hands."

Cole disconnected his call with a smile. "Ivy said everyone's invited to Denver."

"I'm *sure* she did."

Cole ignored Mya's sarcasm and turned to his truck. "Mya and Nat, come. Ivy's packing a suitcase of her clothes for you. I'll call Andre on the way. Rosie, if you want to get a bag packed, Ivy said plan to be gone about ten days."

"Ten days!" Mya squawked.

Jack felt a similar panic bloom in his chest. Gramma and Nat giggled, clapped their hands, and hurried back into Rosie's house to get her ready to bail.

Traitors, all of them.

Mya was pale and refused to look at him. *Fantastic.*

She took a deep breath. "Cole, I'll stay at your place while you guys are partying in Denver."

Her brother thrust a hand through his hair. "No, Mya. I'm only in Denver for two nights, and when I get back to town, I'll be at the fire station for my twenty-four hour shift. The whole idea is for no one to be alone until the police figure out what happened." He turned to look at Jack again. "In fact, I'm starting to think you should stay in the main house instead of the guesthouse, Whiteside. I'd feel better knowing Mya's got eyes on her at all times."

Mya threw her hands up with a rude noise. "Now who's overreacting? We might *never* know if it was random or otherwise," she said.

Jack mentally ran through a series of geologic terms to recenter his fractured emotions. It didn't bother him that she seemed so hostile to the idea of being under the same roof as him.

At least, it shouldn't. "You're right, they might never

know, but it's prudent to take precautions for now," he replied when he was sure his voice would betray no emotion.

Fifteen minutes later, Nat and a still-complaining Mya left with Cole, while Jack and Rosie followed soon after in his rental car to Cole and Ivy's house. After pulling up to the tidy one story, Jackson walked around the car to help Rosie out before getting her luggage from the trunk, but she'd already exited the vehicle. A vibrant wreath adorned Cole and Ivy's front door while pots of flowers every color of the rainbow vied for space on the small portico. It was clearly a well-loved home.

Rosie grasped his arm to make their way up the sidewalk. "The easiest way to take care of Mya is to be her new tango partner."

Jackson froze. *Whoa. What?* "No way, Gramma. I haven't danced in ages."

"Oh, hush. You're such a brilliant man, except when it comes to matters of your own heart. You and Mya were magic on the dance floor and in each other's lives. People can live to be a hundred and never once taste that kind of excitement. Now Artie's injured, and the competition is in a few weeks. If you focus—and I know how focused you can be—the two of you could win that whole blessed thing."

"You know how we left things—"

Rosie stopped just shy of Cole and Ivy's portico and took one of Jack's hands between both of hers. "She still loves you," she whispered.

His heart pounded furiously against his ribcage. *Ridiculous.* "When I told her my dream had finally come true, she slammed the door in my face. We haven't spoken since. You're letting your imagination run away with you."

His gramma's eyes bored up at him. "You and that

beautiful woman are two parts of a whole. Neither one complete without the other." She patted his hand once more, then released it. "I've watched her for two years, trying to move on after you left. She is by nature a happy spirit and full of life, but she lost something that day you all but told her she wasn't as important as your career."

"That's not fair—"

"You, *hush*." She poked a finger in the center of his chest. "It's the same with you, Jack. I've heard it in your voice every time you've called. I've even felt it in your emails. Now, seeing how you look at her and she looks at you even after all this time, it's obvious that you're both still miserable without each other. Love isn't perfect. People aren't perfect. But this could be your second chance."

He tipped his head back and ran a hand through his hair. "This is absurd." Why was he even listening to this nonsense?

"I'm too old for your sass to have any effect, young man. Now what do you say?"

"About what?"

Rosie rolled her eyes. "Kids these days. No attention span. Being her tango partner, what else?"

When he cocked an eyebrow at her, she raised both of her silver ones right back.

There was no way he could be Mya's partner. No fucking way. "We'd end up hurting each other again."

"Stop letting your fear broker your choices. Aspire Athletic—it's that new sporting goods store owned by a retired Broncos linebacker—will sponsor a new dance studio for her if she places in the top three. You left to follow your dream. Now, you could help *her* dream come true."

Rosie took the last few steps to Cole and Ivy's door and

knocked, leaving Jack more unsettled and unsure than he'd been in a couple years. Which should be a flashing sign to stay the hell away from Mya, right? She turned his life upside down without even trying. Months before he'd left the country, he'd grown tired of her empty flirtations orchestrated for the sole purpose of arousing his jealousy. She'd played games with both him and Arturo to try to ease her fear of loss, to make him up his ante—maybe even to make him propose—but he wasn't sure he could ever reassure her enough that he loved her and would never leave her. He felt like she'd never trust his feelings enough to let go of her games.

And that hurt.

But in the end, he'd gone and left her anyway, confirming all her fears.

Their whole relationship was messed up. They'd both made mistakes. Was it worth starting over? Would they be able to change their patterns or would they fall right back into their dysfunctional ways?

When Mya opened Cole and Ivy's front door, no one said anything as Rosie quietly entered the house. When Jack continued to stand there, Mya raised an eyebrow and stepped onto the portico, pausing between two enormous black pots that made her look small and alluringly feminine.

"Well? What are you doing?" she asked.

Thinking about how much I want you. How bad you are for my mental health. "Trying to clear my head."

"You have a clearer head than anyone I've ever met, Jack."

As Mya advanced on him, he focused on his breathing. She smelled like exotic flowers. Images of her satin skin, quivering as he buried his head between her legs, wove around him. She'd screamed for him that night—the night before they'd broken up—and he'd never, *ever* forget the sound. He shifted back a couple of steps until he was on the sidewalk, growing uncomfortable in his khakis. "Everyone getting ready to leave?" he asked.

"Yes. Andre got here shortly after we did. He's going to Denver, too," she replied.

Jack had noticed the extra vehicle in Cole's driveway. "Not you though."

She smiled with her lips only. "The others can afford a week off. I can't. Not with having to find a new partner and the clock ticking before the competition."

They stared at each other as a plump robin sang in the honey locust tree that spread its gauzy canopy on the yard.

"Look, I don't think I should stay with you..." She trailed off.

That glimpse of vulnerability, fleeting though it was, surprised him. Made him want to wrap her up and tell her everything would be okay. He shoved his hands in his slacks. What did she want him to say? Did she want him to beg? "It probably won't be for long. The police should have some answers soon, but in the meantime, I don't want you to be alone *anywhere*. When you're not at dispatch or at the dance studio, you can come to my office at the university. According to my assistant, it's quite spacious." He needed to stop talking. *Now*.

"That's kind of you, Jack, but I don't plan to haunt your office."

Rosie stuck her head out the front door. "We're almost ready to leave. Jack, did you ask her yet?"

Jackson's chest tightened. "Mind you own damn business, Gramma."

"Balderdash. When you're seventy-eight, you get certain liberties. Now ask her."

He would *not* bring it up. Maneuvering the same living space with Mya was going to be torturous enough. Dancing with her, feeling the minute shifts of her muscles as they responded to his own...

Down that road lay madness.

Mya looked slightly ill. "Ask me what?"

"You two would be magnificent tango partners," Rosie said sweetly, before withdrawing back into the house, the door closing with a soft swoosh.

Mya's eyes widened momentarily, then bit her lip.

Oh, shit. She couldn't possibly be weighing the idea. A veil of sweat broke out all over Jack's body as she opened that perfect mouth.

"Well, that's...interesting. It's been two years, but we *were* good together." Her lips parted, and he realized that he wasn't the only one remembering his body joining hers—the wild passion, the slow loving—all of it.

Mya blinked and shook her head as though dismissing the memories. "I know you probably have hard feelings. I do, too. But we could make it strictly about business. I really do need a partner."

Nothing with Mya was ever 'strictly business.' She was too passionate for that. He didn't bother telling her his grandmother had already told him about her goal. Didn't bother telling her he'd never forget her dreams or every little thing that mattered to her.

He'd *never* forget. But he could let her talk, explain, try to convince him. All the while, he knew. Knew he'd never be able to tell her no.

But he wanted to make her sweat it out—at least a little —because he'd have hours of sweating and subsequent cold showers of his own in the coming weeks.

Son of a bitch.

FIVE

He's *gonna refuse.* She could see it in those hypnotic gray-blue eyes, the likes of which she had yet to observe on another living soul. She could see his contrariness in the tensing of his stubbled jaw, the thinning of his lips with their ridiculously sensual curve. She must be mad to have even considered Rosie's idea, much less practically asked Jack to do it. Still, who else was there? Octavian was a possibility, but he was no where near as in tune with her body as Jack had always been.

Would their time apart make a difference? "We could try it. We'd know after an hour if it would work or not," she said. His pupils expanded behind his tortoiseshell frames, his gaze warming instantly. Her belly twirled, her entire body restless with that one simple, dangerous look. She crossed her arms like a shield in front of her, but his eyes still emoted that dark craving. "W-well? Say something. You're deliberately making this harder than it has to be."

"Nothing with you is ever easy, Mya."

His voice had roughened, raising goose bumps up and down her arms. "You used to like that," she whispered.

Neither of them spoke for long moments. Two years seemed to fall away as she lost herself in his eyes. A battle waged in his steady gaze. On the outside, everyone saw a wildly attractive, brilliant scientist. Very few got to know the ardor that beat inside the logical geo-archaeologist. The hunger behind his low-key exterior. She saw it for a brief moment under the blue Colorado sky.

A breeze ruffled his hair. She reached up to smooth it back down, but he grabbed her wrist before her hand could make contact. "I can't do this with you again, Mya."

She blinked hard as tiny spikes drove into the backs of her eyes. "I'm not asking for a relationship. I only need a dance partner. You make the most sense because we already know how to dance together."

"It wouldn't be the same. We were a couple when we danced. In tune with each other. Now, we have all these unresolved feelings. And all of that will surely translate on the dance floor. You should know that better than anyone," he said.

"The tango is the ultimate dance for unresolved feelings."

He swore and started to move around her toward Cole and Ivy's front door.

"Wait! I'm sorry, that was insensitive." When he paused on the sidewalk, she continued, "You took me by surprise. You always seem to have everything figured out. The thought that you still struggle with what happened between us surprises me a little." More like *a lot*.

He frowned. "You were always insecure about my feelings for you. But the fact that you're surprised I didn't move on immediately afterward makes me realize how doomed we actually were."

"Don't say that!" She ran her sweaty hands down the

sides of her shorts. How did she always make such a mess of things? "I didn't mean it like that either. I'm just so much more of a mess than you." She grabbed his hand, because if she had to go without touching him for one more minute she'd expire. "I never wanted to hurt you, Jack. I don't know why I used Artie to make you jealous. I'm trying to change. I don't *want* to make people crazy. *Honestamente.*"

"Why change now, after all this time?"

She sighed and her shoulders drooped. "I don't know. Maybe I finally see how my self-interests have often been at the expense of other people's feelings. Once you see that in yourself, it's hard to forget." She paused, not ready to see confirmation in his eyes. "Makes you feel like a jackass." She was still getting used to the think-before-you-speak thing, but she had to admit, it had saved her butt a few times already.

He remained silent. She raised her gaze to his. His eyes now had an amused glint to them. When he brushed a hand through her messy hair, her heart cartwheeled.

"Good luck finding a partner. I'm sure you'll do well at the competition." He turned away and moved onto the portico before his words even registered.

"What?" She stared at his back. "Are you kidding me? You can't lead me on like that!"

He entered Ivy and Cole's house and closed the door behind him. She muttered several bilingual insults under her breath, knowing all the while she was sliding backwards from all her good intentions. But, whatever. When she caught up to him inside, she already knew all the choice words she'd unleash upon the arrogantly handsome professor.

It was going to be *such* a release.

Her hand twisted the doorknob, but it wouldn't turn.

When she twisted harder, her palm slid across the immobile brass.

The third try was also a bust.

The magnificent *bastardo* had locked her out.

———

JACKSON TOOK a moment in the foyer to compose his disordered, sexually explicit thoughts. Truth was, he was both giddier, and, thanks to the threat to her safety—more wary and on the *qui vive*—than he'd been in ages. Sparring with Mya—actually being able to knock her off balance as much as she did to nearly everyone she came into contact with—was a heady thing.

Locking her out of the house was the *pièce de résistance* of their whole exchange.

Score one for the boring professor.

Until reason returned, bringing with it memories of the riot gas assault this morning. Of course he was going to partner with her so he could keep an eye on her. And so he didn't have to suffer the thought of another man's hands on her body.

He ground his teeth together, praying he'd remember how incompatible they were sooner rather than later.

"Thought I heard someone come in. Did you ask her then?" His gramma peered through the side curtain onto the portico.

Shit. Rosie never missed anything. This was starting to feel like high school, trying to keep his love life private all over again. "Shouldn't you be leaving for Denver?"

Rosie never got a chance to answer. Mya blew into the house by way of the back patio, Spanish insults dropping a hundred knots an hour from her fantasy-inducing lips, leveling everyone in her path. She moved toward him, her lovely mouth spewing abuse. He stood his ground as she came right up in his personal space, certain parts of his anatomy awakening at her nearness. "Don't go away mad, just go away," he said, trying in vain not to smile.

"Uh oh, Jack. That was foolish," Rosie warned pleasantly.

Mya's eyes spit green-gold fire as she used both hands to shove at his chest, pushing him a step back. Before he had a chance to recover, she rammed into him again, and he stumbled backwards briefly. The next time she came at him, he was ready. He grabbed her upper arms, swung her around toward the wall, and pushed her back against the gray grasscloth wallpaper, bending down so they were sharing airspace. "So much for learning to curb your impulses, you little liar."

Rosie tapped his back. "Jack, you're being a brute."

Mya tilted her chin up, her hair catching on the textured wallpaper. "Jerking me around outside wasn't fair!"

"Hear, hear!" Rosie crowed.

Jack bared his teeth. His fingers tightened more on Mya's arms as he swiveled his neck to glare at Rosie. "Gramma, would you Please. Leave us. Alone?" When Rosie disappeared down the hall with an exaggerated sigh, Jack returned his gaze to Mya, steadfastly refusing to look at her mouth. "You spilled your guts outside without so much as a prompt from me, so don't pin this shit on me."

Her lips parted, and of course he looked at them. *Fuck.* His dick surged to life.

"You—" Her mouth snapped shut. Lips pouted. Then frowned. Then looked like she was about to cry.

Oh, Jesus. Now he was the Big Bad Wolf.

His fingers loosened their grip on her arms. A tear beaded up on her thick, black eyelashes. His chest expanded with all those damned soft, messy feelings she stirred up in him. "My*aaa*..."

She snuck her arms up between them, squishing the heels of her hands into her eyes. She sniffed loudly. "You're right. I suck at this." As she lowered her hands, they scuffed against his lower ab wall. He nearly went cross-eyed. "I'm sorry, Jack. I don't blame you for thinking I'm a head case."

"It's fine. You've had a lot to deal with today. Stress can make anyone act like a monster."

She blinked luminous eyes that made him fantasize about bedrooms and satin sheets. "You think I'm a monster?"

"What? *No.* I just meant, well, you know what I mean."

She shook her head and unabashedly yawned. "No, I really don't."

Well, hell. He couldn't remember what he meant either when she was looking at him so languorously. "You haven't been sleeping enough, have you?" The words slipped out before he could stop them. Before they'd dated, she'd confessed that she never slept more than five hours a night. Being with him had been good for her sleep hygiene— middle of the night sexual hijinks notwithstanding. He wondered if she'd reverted to her poor sleep patterns after their breakup.

She yawned again. "I can sleep when I'm dead."

Aha. "We've had this conversation a hundred times, Mya. There are neurocognitive consequences of sleep deprivation. Your prefrontal cortex needs to rest every twenty four hours."

"*Blah, blah, blah.* My gray matter is not your concern anymore, science boy."

"It is if I'm going to be your partner."

She squinted, refocusing on him. "What? I thought you said..."

He was quite enjoying her consternation. "Getting ready for a national competition will take hours. Tell me why I should give up my free time to do this?"

She blinked as though trying to clear away cobwebs of exhaustion. "If we place in the top three, Aspire Athletic is going to sponsor me, providing capital to open a new studio. In addition to regular offerings, I plan to provide free classes to low-income students. You'd be helping make that possible."

"That's still mostly about you. Try again."

"Because you like to dance?"

"I don't even know if that's true anymore."

He stopped breathing when something gave way in her eyes. She lifted a hand to his chest. "I think, deep down, we both wonder if there's still something between us," she whispered.

He swallowed hard. "I wouldn't have to dance with you to discover that."

She shook her head, the black strands shifting across the grasscloth behind her head. "Dancing opens the senses."

He leaned down further. "So does kissing." He pressed his lips to the silken hair by her temple.

She shivered. "Yes."

That simple agreement pleased him inordinately. He smiled and leaned back fractionally to take in her closed eyes, the slightly parted lips, the rapid rise and fall of her chest. *Exquisite.* He widened his stance and placed his forearms beside her head, leaned down, and felt the walls concuss when their lips met. She opened to him, and they both inhaled in wonder. The gentle give of her lips, feathery soft. Her body pliant and lush. The sensation of falling into her even as his body expanded. Made him drunk and disoriented, invincible and filled with clarity.

Her fingers, palms, arms, and legs sought his skin, rubbing against him with an earthiness that he had yet to find an equal in any other woman. She tugged off his glasses, pulled his head down, and kissed his eyelids, his cheekbones. *Yes.* He recognized her. He'd missed this. The years between them dissolved, and here she was again, the missing piece that challenged, annihilated, and then reordered him with such precision.

Her jaw fit perfectly in his hand as he held her in place. Kissing, tasting, exploring the fragrant spot where her pulse beat in her neck. The wall underneath his palm shook again, and Mya stiffened, then lifted her chin to break his hold, then froze. *What?*

"Ah shit, you guys, my *eyes*! Get a fucking room."

"Andre! Language!" Mya scolded.

Jackson followed Mya's gaze to the five bodies squeezed in the hall beyond the foyer. Andre shook his head with a disgusted look, gave them the bird, and turned back down the hallway in a rapid retreat.

Rosie was smirking in a decidedly non-grandmotherly way. "Things were just starting to get interesting! Don't mind us, lovebirds. Please do carry on!" she singsonged.

"Not cool, Gramma." How the hell was he going to turn around with this monster erection?

Nat giggled. "Naw, you're cool, Rosie."

Ivy wrapped one arm around Cole's waist and draped the other around Nat's shoulders. "Well, then, shall we get going and leave them to it?" She smiled at Jack and Mya. "Feel free to stay as long as you like. Guest bedroom and laundry are both down the hall to the right. Just lock up when you leave."

Jack felt tongue-tied. Mya wasn't saying anything either, which was exceptionally unusual, and this disorderly intimate-human-relations-caught-in-the-act stuff was *not* his territory.

And he still couldn't turn around.

Mya wiggled against his erection. He nearly swallowed his tongue. When he looked down at her, she was smirking.

"You're trouble with a capital T," he whispered.

"Good thing you enjoy puzzles, *hombre*." She ducked under his arms and went to hug her family goodbye. Cole gathered everyone's luggage, told Mya she wasn't allowed to use his truck, then herded Ivy, Rosie, Andre, and Nat into Ivy's car.

Soon enough, the house was quiet, and the wicked thoughts started rolling through Jack's mind....

The feel of Mya's thighs parting, the delicate pink of her nipples...

Ivy *had* invited them to use the bedroom.

Don't be rash. Mya had enough of that particular trait for both of them.

But God, they were good together. Sex didn't have to be complicated.

Yeeeeeah, right.

"Earth to Jackson."

His eyes refocused on the Cuban beauty in front of him. Her smile was perhaps the most saccharine he'd ever seen on her. His senses went on instant alert.

"So...about that dance partnership...?"

"You can save your ingratiating smiles, Mya. They have no power over me." *Liar.* "However, I will consent to *testing out* a partnership—"

She squealed and threw herself at him in one of her monkey hugs, all boa-constrictor arms around his neck, her toned, dancer legs wrapped around his trunk. His hands found her ass like they were equipped with a homing device.

"Thank you, thank you, *thank you,* Jack. I *know* we can do this. I promise to be good." Her words dropped fervently against his neck, making his heart race and his body seethe with tension.

His fingers curled into the taut muscles of her butt, lifting her against him until he felt her gasp. "I didn't commit yet. We'll have to see how it goes." He had to make sure she knew this was merely a trial.

And he only had about another twenty seconds of coherence with the way she was starting to grind against him.

"*Lo sé*, s'okay," she breathed.

He started walking to the guest bedroom, his thoughts fracturing. "And only if you promise you'll stay close by until the police figure out if this was a targeted attack. I mean it, Mya."

Her head popped up from where her lips had been fused to his earlobe. "I will not be kept, Jack."

He paused in the middle of the hallway because he couldn't be mobile and get his brain firing with enough agility to handle Mya's objections at the same time. "I'm not suggesting a 'kept' arrangement. I'm only proposing a logical solution."

She smiled and kissed him flat on the mouth, short circuiting his synapses. When she lifted her head, her eyes had that warm glow he'd remembered a thousand nights, lying alone in his tent.

"I'll be fine at Rosie's whether you're there or not. The

only other places I'll be are at work or the gym practicing with you or training a new group of students." She wriggled out of his arms and patted his cheek. "You are a lovely man. I'll cook you *ropa vieja y frijoles negro con arroz* to show my appreciation. See you at Rosie's later! *Adios!*"

She grabbed her brother's off-limit keys from a hook next to the garage door.

"Mya, wait! It's not safe to go out alone—"

She squealed Cole's truck tires backing out of the garage. Jackson closed the garage door, locked up, and walked back to his rental car parked at the curb trying not to think about someone who might possibly mean her ill will.

Or the risk he was taking with his own heart and sanity.

SIX

Mya loved Rosie's kitchen. The rest of the home needed massive updating, but this tiny, bright space was perfection with its white cabinets, black granite counter tops, glossy white subway tiles, and windows that kissed the home's nine foot ceilings. She set three grocery bags on the counter, then peeled off the yellow post-it note attached to the stainless steel refrigerator.

You are in trouble, little lady. Make sure all doors are locked, then call me. Immediately.

So bossy. Jack had obviously come here looking for her after she'd left Cole and Ivy's, but she'd stopped at the hospital to check on Artie. Seeing his eyes wrapped in gauze shook her up more than she'd been this morning when everything had gone down. The doctors had performed some serious ocular irrigation to flush out residual CS particles and had discovered some corneal abrasion, but they were hopeful he'd recover without any permanent vision loss.

Please make it so.

Instead of calling Jack—she did *not* feel like a lecture—

she texted her *all's well* to the number he provided, then turned on the radio and arranged the ingredients for *ropa vieja* and black beans with rice next to the stove. After changing into yoga pants and a tank top she'd borrowed from Ivy, she poured a glass of wine.

She could hardly wait until Jack got home. He'd texted back saying he'd checked in at the university. But he hadn't said when he'd be back.

Don't start depending on him.

After a few days, she could stay with Cole. She *should* stay with him, but...

She'd rather stay with Jack. She wasn't even going to question her reasons. She'd get through this disturbing home invasion thing, then deal with her feelings about Jack. Rosie had said the university wanted to keep him longer than a year, but so far, he'd only committed to one.

She needed to remember that. And stay on alert in case someone wanted to hurt her.

She heated a Dutch oven, coated the pan with oil, and added two flank steaks. Besides the drug felons who maybe blamed her for their incarceration, who else could be angry enough with her to attempt this kind of attack? A few parents had pulled their kids out of dance lessons last month, but that had been due to conflicts with the gym where she was currently teaching, not any beef they had with her.

She added onion, peppers, and garlic to the pan. Forty-five minutes later, she had the beans prepped when the front door opened. A smile tugged at her mouth and her shoulders unwound. She poured a second glass of wine, and took it with her as she headed into the living room. "I've been wait—"

She stopped mid-stride as Jack stepped back, allowing a

tall blonde to precede him into the room. The woman was startlingly attractive in a make-up-free, pale, northern European way.

And physically, the polar opposite of Mya.

She set the wine glass on an end table and met Jackson's eyes.

"You clearly didn't receive my text," he said, the expression in his eyes unreadable. "This is my colleague, Dr. Lilith Erickson. We met at a symposium at Stanford and have consulted on multiple projects over the years. Her expertise is environmental isotope geochemistry, but her main interest is paleohydrology. She's the one who lobbied to bring me to CSU."

How nice. Mya was self-aware enough to realize that Jackson was overcompensating for the sudden awkwardness in the room by continuing to talk, but Jesus, *isotope paleo-whatever?* Something to do with water and chemistry, obviously.

Could she feel any more deficient? She'd only attended one year of technical college before she decided to start earning money doing the dispatch thing so she could start a college fund for Nat and Andre and set something aside for a dance studio of her own. How could she have forgotten the scholarly circles Jack ran in? After two years of working with world-renown archeologists on a high-profile excavation, she would probably bore him to tears with her plebeian talk.

After Jack fell silent, Mya stepped forward to shake the brilliant and beautiful geochemist's hand. "Nice to meet you, Dr. Erickson. Will you stay for supper? It should be ready in another half hour or so." *You can enlighten me about things I won't understand, and I can watch you and*

Jack laugh with your insider geology jokes. Won't that be fabulous?

"Please, call me Lilith." The woman's voice was deeper than Mya expected. Elegant, yet warm. Like her hands, though they were slightly rough against Mya's own. "And thank you for the offer, but I only stopped by to borrow Jackson's new structural compass for a demonstration I'm giving tomorrow at a field luncheon."

Oh, just one of those. Whatever the hell a structural compass did, it couldn't possibly rock a man's world as much as Dr. Erickson's gorgeous blue eyes, model-perfect lips, and cheeks that could chisel diamonds. The contrast between the woman's looks and her work-rough hands was interesting and somehow threatening.

And she was *nice. Damn.*

"In the chaos of this morning, I forgot to bring the compass to the office," Jack supplied.

"I see. Sounds interesting. Well, I'll just leave you two to your tools, then." *Ai, yai, yai.* Mya rolled her eyes at her shallow self as she grabbed the single wine glass and returned to the kitchen. She stirred the beans and rice and turned up the music to drown out the timbre of the scientists' voices from the other room. Jack and Lilith were obviously well acquainted if Lilith was the one who made room for Jack in the university's geological sciences department.

But how well acquainted? Had they ever been lovers? When she and Jack were together, he'd never once mentioned Lilith. What did that mean?

Stop. It was none of her business.

She swore when the shredded meat started burning. Moments later Jack came into the kitchen.

"That smells amazing. I skipped lunch. I suppose you did, too, with everything that happened."

She looked over her shoulder at him as she continued to stir the meat. "She's gone already?"

"She only came for the compass."

Mya bit her lip, trying not to look relieved. "You really should have had her stay. I wouldn't have minded. I'm sure you two have a lot of catching up to do, unless you've stayed in touch..."

He leaned a hip against his grandmother's counter and reached for the glass of wine she'd poured for him earlier. "You're fishing for information. Why?"

"I'm not fishing." Oh hell, she totally was, and she could never, ever hide shit from him so she might as well dump it out there and be done with it. "Were you two ever lovers?"

Jack paused mid-swallow, raising an eyebrow. He set the glass down. "And this is your business because...?"

She frowned and stabbed at the pile of meat. Maybe she should burn the damn thing after all. "Well, if you plan to bring her here for the night..." *For a hot sweaty interlude. Ugh!* "It kinda does affect me. Like, I need to know if I should buy some heavy duty ear plugs, or not be here during a certain witching hour, or something." Her *ropa vieja* recipe had never seen beef shredded to this degree. With every stab and shred, she swore a different foul word in her head. And when she exhausted her Spanish vocabulary, she started in on English.

And he still didn't say shit.

She couldn't do this. She'd been in his presence for less than a day and already he'd turned her inside out. And she'd let him do it.

Soy muy estupido.

She turned off the burners for the meat, rice, and beans,

then pivoted away from where he was standing, a slight up-tilt to his lips.

"I'm not hungry anymore. Thanks for the offer, but I'll find another place to stay," she said.

He grabbed her arm before she could take two steps. He was deceptively fast for such a big man. "*Mya.*"

Ooo, when her name dropped like that in his smooth, cultured bass. Like a caress. "Don't say it like that," she snapped.

"Why, when you like it so much?"

"I don't. Not anymore."

"You're a terrible liar. And so easy to rile."

"I'm glad I'm entertaining to someone of your vast intelligence and academic repute. Now, goodbye."

He spun her back around and his lips came down on hers, hard, hot, and demanding. She opened to him, gasping into his mouth, all the pent up emotion of the day released in a flood, leaving her quaking at his invasion. His palms cupped her ass, parting her legs, dragging her up his body over his rigid erection as he turned and slid her onto the counter top. "Damn you, Mya. How can you unravel me so easily?"

She couldn't breathe with his lips, teeth, mouth branding her neck so possessively. Couldn't gather her thoughts. Didn't want to think. His thumbs brushed the undersides of her breasts, fingers tightening reflexively on her ribs, and her head arced back on a long, shuddering sigh, her legs wrapping around his trunk to draw him closer. *Madre de dios*, he was solid.

She thrust her fingers into his silky hair, pulling, making him growl and rise from her neck to slide his glasses on the counter before claiming her lips again. She tasted the rich cabernet on his tongue, the wine's deep complexity adding another layer of seduction. She shivered when his fingers trailed slowly down her body, such a contrast with his busy mouth, to stop at the hem of her cotton tank top. He leaned back to pull her shirt by the hem, over her head, then chucked it on the floor. His eyes, the deep blue of a stormy Caribbean Sea, spoke of a yearning that knew no relief. She stripped off his polo and pulled him to her, shaking now with something stronger than lust. His mouth slanted against hers, slower now, his fingertips like butterfly wings against her belly, tracing aching circles around her belly button, until they edged under the waistband of her yoga pants.

"*Jack.*"

His fingers slipped beneath the satin of her thong, rubbing, pressing...

Remembering.

"God, Mya. I've always loved making you come undone like this," he groaned, his mouth wet and erotic at her ear as his fingers played her like they always had. His skin was a love song against hers, warm and poignant with memories. Her legs trembled, widened, shifted. Her heart throbbed, her breasts ached. His other hand splayed across her back, and she shook so hard she thought she'd lose the rhythm. The cord was winding tighter within. She moaned louder now, her hips rolling on the granite in time to his hand at her center. He was her world. His colors, his scent, taste, texture. She loved his skin. *Loved it.*

So different from hers.

"That's it, come for me," he whispered hoarsely against her mouth.

She bit his lower lip as her body convulsed, bowing into his. He murmured incomprehensible words, his hand continuing to pleasure her, not letting her down easily, until she wrapped her arms around his neck, burying her face against the pulse that raced there, desperately trying to hold back the tears that had risen unbidden to her eyes.

Such a release, it overwhelmed her.

Jackson held her, unspeaking, stroking her hair as her breathing returned to normal. Felt so good. She never wanted to leave his arms, but it was up to her to make the next move. She blinked, her eyelashes brushing against the sensitive skin under his ear. He shivered.

Do something, Castillo.

Finally, she pulled back and was about to raise a hand to touch his lips, ready for whatever happened next, but he took a step back, cleared his throat, and ran a hand through the hair that her hands had pulled so insistently. His eyes darkened again as they raked over her passion-warmed body, making her sex respond immediately.

But instead of coming back for round two, he reached for his glasses and slid them onto the bridge of his nose, not quite managing to suppress a shiver. "Well, the chemistry's still there. We should do alright in the competition."

Then he dished up a plate of *ropa vieja*, black beans, and rice and sat down at Rosie's table like he hadn't just given her the most body-quaking orgasm she'd had since the day he left her sheets.

SEVEN

Jack didn't see any lights on in his gramma's living room as Lilith pulled her Subaru into Rosie's driveway. Part of him was relieved that Mya had obviously gone through with her plan to visit her siblings in Denver after her dispatch shift. But another part...

It was getting ridiculous how much he'd been thinking about her in the last week since he'd returned. Of course, it didn't help that she was usually within arms' reach. Or that all her vibes projected her openness to him. *Just kiss her.* How often had he been *this close* to following the urgings of his body. But he'd planned for this reaction to her. What he *hadn't* planned on was her living with him. Lying down in bed with only a thin wall separating him from the object of his obsession. Her orange-blossom shampoo in the shower, her socks strewn around the house, her spoon in the yogurt in the refrigerator.

Since the police hadn't been able to find evidence of a targeted attack against Mya and the week had been uneventful, he'd been spending more time away from home to save his sanity. But of course, that only increased his distraction because when she wasn't with him, he was wondering where she was and what she was doing and if she was safe.

Which was markedly neurotic and decidedly stalkerish.

Two states of mind he would've never thought himself capable.

So, tonight he'd decided to go out with colleagues after a meeting. Mya wasn't going to be home anyway. After a few drinks, he left the restaurant, only to find his truck tires had been slashed. After he reported the incident and had his truck towed to the tire shop, Lilith had graciously offered to bring him home.

She turned to face him, leaving her car running. "I'm glad you decided to join us tonight. A few people have commented about your distractedness of late. Are you second guessing your position here?" she asked.

He shook his head. "Not at all. I apologize." He didn't like sharing his private life, even with people he regularly worked with. "I just need to resolve some personal issues that have cropped up since returning home."

"You may need to start compartmentalizing a little more effectively. We need you firing on all cylinders once classes begin."

He nodded and glanced again at the front windows, dreading the thought of being alone with his thoughts of Mya. "You're right. Why don't you come in for a couple of minutes? I'll share some of Mya's famous sangria and show you the documentation for my Wadi Murabba'at Caves paper so you'll stop hounding me."

Lilith laughed. "I'll never stop pestering you for glimpses into your brilliant mind." She turned off the engine. "Sangria and documentation, what could be more compelling?"

He got out and closed the passenger door. "How about more graduate fellows with the enthusiasm of your highly-touted Ms. Hollows?"

Lilith followed him up the walkway to the front door. "Timber Hollows is a godsend. You'll meet her soon. She lives, breathes, and sleeps geochemistry. And she keeps our accreditation paperwork zealously organized. She's definitely making me look good to the Board."

When Jack unlocked the front door, loud crooning strains of Justin Timberlake streamed from the kitchen. His heart slid into his throat almost in slow motion. *She's home.* His breath eased, sliding in a deep exhale between his slightly parted lips that curled up in spite of himself.

He shut the door with a soft click behind Lilith, knowing he probably should have slammed it to alert Mya he was home. "Come on back to the kitchen. We'll say hi to Mya, get some sangria, then I'll grab my papers."

He led the way to his grandmother's cozy kitchen, his heart rate increasing with every step. He rounded the corner and pulled up short, his gaze arrested by the fetching picture Mya presented, perched on the counter top, feet in the sink. She wore a strapless red dress, the skirt voluminous, splayed out, draping down the lower cabinets as she painted her toenails a vibrant crimson to match the dress. Her long black hair curved across one shoulder, curled just so, caressing her cheek in a flawless waving style like glamorous movie stars from the forties.

And her cleavage as she bent over her legs to apply the polish...

He swallowed hard.

She glanced up and sent him a red-lipped smile that nearly turned him into a babbling fool. Her gaze went over his shoulder. "Hi Lilith, I was hoping you'd stop by again one of these days. Jack, where are your manners? Do step aside so your guest doesn't have to peer over your shoulder."

He shifted, not sure he should be vocalizing, but, "why are you doing that in the sink? Don't most people paint their toes on the floor or a chair?"

Mya raised an eyebrow and put another coat on the toes he'd fantasized sucking way too much for his peace of mind lately. "Guess I'm not most people," she said.

"Where are you going dressed like that?"

Mya sent him a devilish smile and screwed on the top of the red polish. "Wouldn't you like to know?"

Lilith laughed. "Way to make him sweat. I'll have you know he's been offering your sangria for bribery."

Mya smiled and lifted her feet out of the sink, letting them dangle over the cabinets. "Is that so?" She brought her amused gaze to Jack. "What are you hoping to gain with your bribe, Professor?"

Right now? Time alone with her. He'd give Lilith the entire pitcher to make her leave. "It wasn't bribery, it was gratitude. My tires were slashed downtown. Lilith gave me a ride home."

"Yours were the only ones?" When Jack nodded, Mya frowned. "That sucks. Classes haven't even started and you've already managed to piss people off. Not a good sign, smart guy." She eased down from the counter and went to the fridge. Jack's gaze fell on a thick textbook that had been hidden behind her skirts. *An Introduction to Geoarchaeology*. It was a substantial book written by a well-respected, professor emeritus of geoarchaeology and archaeology at Boston University. Mya bustled around, watching him, but pretending not to as she removed the sangria, pulled out three glasses and filled them. Her emotions were so easy to read, yet so complex. Like layers of the earth that told the story of its creation.

I love that about her.

He wandered over to the textbook, noticing the dog-eared pages even before he opened it up to find large blocks of text highlighted in various shades of pink, orange, yellow, and blue. A curious lightness settled in his chest.

Mya handed the first glass to Lilith, pausing when she noticed Jack holding up the textbook. He smiled. She bit her lower lip.

"If you want to sit in on one of my classes, all you have to do is say the word." *I'll even give you private lessons.*

She seemed to regain her footing when she shrugged and handed him a glass of the refreshing berry and brandy-infused wine. "I figured it wouldn't hurt to know a little about what you're up to all day, especially when you constantly badger me to hang out at the college. And honestly, how irritating is it when someone does Sudoku puzzles in ink, for god's sake? I gotta do something to up my game, right?"

Lil hummed her approval of both Mya's commentary as well as the sangria. "He's still doing that? I agree, very annoying."

Jack interpreted Mya's fiercely downward pulling brows to mean she didn't like Lil knowing about his Sudoku proclivities. It suggested a sort of intimacy, he supposed, but she was getting way ahead of herself, thinking he and Lil had been lovers. This was probably going to degenerate. He should've told Mya that first day that he and Lil had never been lovers. Lil had been interested once upon a time, but that time had long since passed. She was attractive, but they were too much alike to hold each other's interest.

There was also the fact that he was strung out over a fragrant Latina flower he couldn't exorcise from his mind.

"What about the tear gas? Have the police ascertained any leads on the attack?" Lilith asked, pulling her phone out of her pocket.

Mya sighed and set her glass on the counter. He could read her inner fight to be nice when she wanted to strike out in her frustration, wondering about him and Lil. He was going to tell her the truth tonight so there would be one less thing between them. No more *should have dones*.

"So far they've turned up nothing. They're pretty sure it was a case of wrong-place-wrong-time for Artie. The thief could've decided to break into anyone's house. That's the good news. The shitty part is that I'm still waiting for the cleanup team to blow out all the toxins from my HVAC system so I can go back home."

Maybe he'd call up the service and pay them to keep putting Mya off.

"I can see why you'd...be...frustrated." Lil's voice faded off as she became preoccupied with her phone.

Mya's gaze jumped between Lil and Jack several times as though silently asking him what had caused the change in Lilith's disposition. For several days now something had been off with Dr. Erickson, but he hadn't had time to ask her about it. Besides it would have been awkward since their relationship had never skewed that way before. Still, she seemed withdrawn periodically, enough that it was definitely noticeable.

"Well, you kids have fun. If you drink the whole bottle, call her a cab." Mya stretched sinuously, and it was all Jack could do to keep his eyes off her neckline where her breasts rose temptingly. "I'm going to bed. 'Night."

What? He would've been relieved she was going to bed

if he didn't suspect she'd sneak out the window, dressed to the nines as she was. It had been one of her favorite teenage rebellion activities. And he'd always been the one to bring her back home. "You don't look or act like you're ready for bed."

As soon as he said the words, he realized how sexually charged they sounded. He didn't dare break eye contact with Mya to gauge Lil's reaction. Besides, at this point, he didn't care what Dr. Erickson might speculate.

"Oh really? And how do I look when I'm ready to go to bed, Jack?"

A loaded question he'd sincerely love to answer. But not with a colleague in the room. "You're dressed like you're ready to walk a runway. And you just did your toes. You'll get them all smudged up if you go to bed right now."

"Since when are you the toenail fashion expert? And why do you even care? There's no impending threat to me, and we're not a thing, so what's the deal?"

His face heated, but Lilith discretely left the kitchen, saving him more disgrace. "Dammit, Mya." He was at a loss.

"Dammit, what? You're always pissed at me, but I never really know why exactly. Unless you just can't stand my face. Is that it?"

She approached him, barefoot on the tile, those newly-painted red toes peeking out from under her flouncy skirt. Her eyes snapped a challenge he chomped at the bit to accept.

Don't. He was a man of logic. This trading of insults was merely a matter of heightened estrogen and testosterone. He could give into the sex hormones, haul Mya over her shoulder, fuck her senseless, Lil be damned...

Or he could save professional face and take one more goddamn cold shower later.

He raised his hand to rub his thumb across her generous lower lip, then immediately dropped his arm again. "If you sneak out of this house, I'll find you and lock you in the next time."

He left her standing there and returned to Lil in his gramma's cozy, outdated living room, knowing it had been the wrong thing to say.

Wrong, wrong, wrong.

But he meant every illogical word.

EIGHT

J ackson pivoted, then dipped Mya as the dark gray walls of the dance studio absorbed the final beat of the music. The dimmed crystal chandelier above them cast a golden hue on Mya's neck where her pulse beat a staccato rhythm from the rigors of the dance routine. The tango—jealous lover that it was—had demanded intimacy between them for two weeks now. Ever since he'd threatened to lock her in the house, she'd been diligently ignoring him, their unavoidable interactions at Rosie's house cool and professional.

But once they stepped onto the dance floor, how quickly their bodies remembered one another.

Before their very first hour back on the hardwood floor, Jack had made but a single request. Mya couldn't use the song she'd intended to dance with Arturo. She went one step further by re-choreographing the entire routine extemporaneously that first night. She'd always been a brilliant, intuitive choreographer, but now she seemed to translate a song's notes into kinetic artistry. A melding of body science and creativity that fascinated him beyond reason.

The tango was a complicated, intricate dance that plunged him into the deep end of his emotions. Intense, sensual, hypnotic.

Oh, and they were *good* together.

He hauled her up to a standing position in the now-quiet space, and tried, for the thousandth time in the last fourteen days, to ignore the vivacious appeal in her eyes. Dancing was like making love. The anticipation of the act, the buildup, the meeting and melding of bodies as they communicated a language all their own. The extravagance of movement...lead, follow, draw together, oppose.

The bonding and release.

Mya sifted through his fingertips like the silk kaftans he'd admired in Moroccan markets, exotic and beautiful.

She turned off the speakers and gracefully floated down to sit on the wooden bench to remove her strappy dancing shoes. The outer rooms beyond the studio were dark and silent. Everyone else had gone home.

She glanced up at him, her sexy dimples peeking out to captivate him. "We're ahead of my expectations. I'm so relieved. You remember all the combinations as though two years haven't intervened. You sure you haven't been dancing by the Dead Sea?"

He smiled back, longing to lift the slightly damp hair at her neck to place his lips there. "No dancing. Not even much music. Working outside makes it tough, especially when everyone likes something different. Playing music just causes arguments." *And makes me think of you.* Silence made it far easier not to remember.

"I couldn't imagine living without music." She shivered

and stood in front of the large studio mirrors, looking like she was working up the confidence to ask him something.

He took a shallow breath. "What is it?"

"A few of us are meeting at Catwalk in about a half hour if you'd like to join us. You've been spending every minute here with me or at school. Cutting loose is good for you. I dare say it'd make you even more successful in all your other pursuits." She shoved her shoes in her bag, then sent him a sassy smile that made his heart flip-flop in his chest.

He glanced at his watch because he couldn't stare at her pretty red lips one more minute and expect to make good decisions. "I have to put together a course syllabus."

"*Pfft!* Classes don't start for another month, so that's no excuse. Come along, you'll get to heckle the drunk co-eds if nothing else entertains you."

Just say no. He deserved a fucking medal for being around Mya as much as he already had these past two weeks without kissing her, much less hauling her off to bed. Her soft hand in his, trusting him to guide her from pivot to *enrosque* into *lapiz*. Her sinuous thigh curving around his planted leg in the *gancho*. The carnal slide of her body with every heartbeat... *Heaven and Hell.* "I'm tired. Maybe next time."

He nearly didn't see her disappointment as she quickly leaned down to gather her sports bag. "Okay, but, if you change your mind, you know where we'll be."

Yeah, at a bar, wearing those skin-tight pants and off-the shoulder top. "I'll drop you off at the door." She'd grown lax about her safety in the last week since no other incidents had occurred, and the police had all but ruled it a random attempted robbery.

"I still have the keychain mace you gave me, and it's

always well-lit around Catwalk. Besides, if anyone's been casing my place, they know by now I'm staying right next door. They've had plenty of time to put another nefarious plan into play, yet nothing's happened. I can't live my life in fear, Jack. I hope you understand that."

He did, but he wasn't ready for her to return to her house when the remediation crew finished up on Monday. His palm tightened on the strap of his own bag as he looked where she stood in the shadows by the doorway. He admired the stubborn set of her jaw even as his chest tightened because of it. She always aroused two opposing feelings in him. How the hell did he deal with that?

"Jack?" Her soft voice reached across the space, intimate and vulnerable suddenly.

"I don't like worrying about you." It was out before he could stop the words.

A small crease appeared between the wings of her black brows. "Then don't. No one has ever been able to make you do anything you didn't want to do. I can't imagine that would change now."

She'd taken his words as an insult when he'd meant the exact opposite. A confession of his inability to remain immune to her. "I can't help it, Mya," he whispered, certain she had no idea what he was really telling her. *You move me to act, to feel—deeply—even when I don't want to.*

Then her mouth opened, her lips drawing apart, the only motion of her body. He felt her uncertainty at what she thought she'd heard—understood—in his quiet statement. Wasn't sure whether he wanted her to translate it or not. Honesty had always been paramount. Honesty in his work, his relationships, his approach to seeing the world and the people who populated it.

Honesty—truth—was the only way out of darkness.

"Seems to me, all you need to do is remember how you walked away two years ago. You didn't worry then, you needn't worry now. I'm older, wiser...meaner."

One second she was there, the next she was gone, leaving him bereft in the middle of the dance floor.

NINE

Mya was ready to rabble rouse. Two excruciatingly long, sexually frustrating weeks of being in Jackson's arms and waiting—just freakin' *waiting*—for him to make a move.

But just...*nothin'*.

She'd seen his desire, had felt it radiating from every pore of his sun-kissed skin, and knew deep in her bones he was constantly riding the edge of something dark and hot. But his infernal control wouldn't give either of them the satisfaction their bodies hungered for.

How she *craved* that man. Hell, yes, craved, yearned... *Coveted*.

She *had* to get rid of some of this pent-up energy or she was either gonna crawl between Jackson's sheets tonight or *die*.

And damned if her pride would let her be the one to crumble. After all, *he* was the one who'd left. If he wanted her, he'd have to man up.

Mya lifted her arms, snapped her fingers, and rolled her hips to the pumping beat coming out of the speakers at

Catwalk, a gritty bar in Fort Collins's famed downtown area, aptly named Old Town. The CSU crowd on Catwalk's bar stools gazed up at her and whooped as she danced all-out on the concrete counter tops. Felt *sooo* good. She smiled at Catwalk's owner, Brett Buck, who winked at her from behind the bar. Then she shimmied over to the stool where her best friend Jasmine was seated, wide-eyed, sipping her third, *I'm-going-to-hate-myself-in-the-morning* martini.

Mya reached her hand toward the shy, stunning brunette who'd been her confidante since the first grade. "Jazzy, *come*. These fellas wanna see your long legs in action up here, too. Right, boys?"

The rowdy group of men leered and hooted their agreement. Jasmine Bradley paled and shook her head vehemently. As usual, Mya wasn't about to pay her reticence any mind. Jazzy never initiated hijinks, but she *always* copped to having fun afterwards. Mya slid Jasmine's drink further down the bar with her foot, then twerked her way into a squat. "Jazzy, my gorgeous yoga master, you *will* get your very fine ass up here with me, or I'll spill to your mom and dad you were sleazing it up with that heavy metal band's drummer instead of attending that yoga retreat last month."

"You wouldn't!" But the look in Jasmine's chocolate brown eyes said she had no doubt Mya would.

Mya raised an eyebrow, then stood to make room for Jazz.

"I hate when you do shit like this," Jasmine muttered.

Mya smiled. "You're not alone, *cariña*."

Jasmine grasped Mya's hand in a death grip and climbed up to the bar, more graceful than she'd ever realize. Jazzy's scars ran soul-deep, damaged by her poor excuse for biological parents before her foster family had literally saved her life when she was eight. If Mya ever met Jasmine's biological family face to face, she'd end up in jail.

Very likely prison.

Maybe even the electric chair.

Mya squeezed Jasmine's hand, wishing for the thousandth time that she could erase every horrific memory that haunted Jazzy in the loneliest hours of the night.

Mya eased slightly behind, slightly perpendicular to Jasmine, putting her hands on the taller woman's slowly rolling hips. "That's it, Jazz. You're a natural, see?"

The corners of Jasmine's lips lifted. When a man tried to grab her ankle, she chuckled in her low-toned, sexy way until she teetered, gasped, and grabbed the cord of one of the exposed-bulb, industrial lamps that hung at intervals over the bar. "*Whoa.*" She hiccuped. "Those three martinis are starting to make the room spin."

Mya steadied her. "Let's sit you down, sweetheart." She kicked the arms of the wanna-be cowboy with a ten gallon hat who'd rattled Jasmine's confidence, then looked back behind the bar. "Buck!"

Brett Buck flipped a towel over his massive shoulder and stalked over, owning every bit of his ex-MMA fighter cred as his *don't-fuck-with-me-or-my-crib* gaze narrowed on the blanching cowboy. "We got trouble over here?"

Urban Cowboy's eyes widened. "Nope. None at all. I's just...I was...leaving—" His seat was vacated and immediately taken by a girl in short shorts and a mid-riff baring t-shirt with Greek symbols.

Brett's glower melted into the devilish grin that scored him more phone numbers than he could follow up in one lifetime. "We good?"

Mya blew him a kiss, then lost herself in the next song,

grinding with Jazzy until something in the murky darkness of the bar's entryway made her belly flutter and the skin on the back of her neck tingle. She held her breath, but continued to move, all her senses honed in on the doorway.

Jack emerged in the golden glow of the room, all tall and freshly-showered, but still five o'clock-shadowed and devastatingly masculine in a simple button-down shirt and jeans.

His gaze locked on her immediately and didn't let up until he took his seat at the very end of the bar. He'd changed his mind. Now what was she supposed to do? She moved and swayed and gave her body over to the song, knowing he was watching her with hungry eyes, making her skin tremble and heart thump dramatically.

"Told you he'd come." Jazzy's brown eyes were finally relaxed.

"Doesn't mean anything," Mya said.

"Oh girl, you're wrong. Now it's your move." Jazz wrapped her arms around Mya and rocked her back and forth. "I want you to be happy."

A brief commotion on the barstools registered moments before Mya went weightless. A male college student's lap reared into her vision, then came a growl, a thud of knuckles meeting flesh-clad bones, and then Mya was grabbed and plopped back upon the counter on her ass. She pushed her hair out of her eyes. Jackson's broad back partially blocked her view of some poor bastard now prone on the black concrete floor, his cowboy hat upside down near Jack's boots.

Jack grabbed the fresh-faced younger man by his CSU Rams shirt-front and hauled him to his feet as Brett came around the bar with a glower that didn't bode well for anyone's health. Mya scooted off the bar, ready to put herself in Brett's path if he was planning to throw down with Jack for raising hell in his bar. The music seemed even louder than before, the bass beat pounding in her neck.

Lordy, Jack smelled incredible, though. Bewitching notes of bergamot, neroli, warm Indonesian patchouli, persimmon, and green tangerine. A heavenly, masculine combination that he knew she'd always loved.

He hadn't worn it one time in the last two weeks. What it might mean that he did so tonight, made her weak in the knees.

"What the f-f-fuck, man?" the student yelled. His hooked nose was bleeding, his eyes darting around the room. Anywhere but at Jack's face.

"You owe these ladies an apology. And you'd better get started *right now*." Jack's big hand twisted harder on the younger man's shirt, the material constricting his throat.

Brett frowned at Mya, then shook his head and brushed her aside to stand next to Jack, crossing his arms over his massive chest, adding a heaping dose of intimidation to Jack's ready-to-kill stance. Looking at the burly, tattooed barkeep, the kid's two preppy pals sat back down in their seats.

Rams t-shirt guy coughed, then wheezed. Jack loosened his grip slightly so he could breathe.

"Yeah, sorry, man. Sorry, I'll never do it again!"

"Don't tell *me*, you imbecile." Jack swiveled toward Mya and Jasmine, hauling the man around like he was a puppet. "Tell *them*."

"Sorry, lady." His gaze moved rapidly from Mya to Jasmine. "Sorry. I'll n-never do it again."

The man looked so humiliated and defeated Mya almost felt sorry for him. She put a hand on Jack's back, his muscles like iron under her fingertips. "Jack, it's okay. He didn't hurt me or Jazz, and he probably didn't mean anything by it."

Jack's eyes burned briefly into hers. "You don't have a Y chromosome, Mya. He sure as hell meant something by tumbling you into his lap." He changed his hold on the man to the back of his shirt and pulled him toward the exit, the poor guy's feet scrambling for purchase. Brett returned to his station behind the bar, but Mya ran after Jack in case he lost his shit outside.

Jack dropped his hold on the man next to the curb. "Don't you *ever* touch another woman without her permission."

"Yeah, okay, whatever," the student cocked off now that Jack's hands weren't on him.

"*Que chingados! Besame el culo, pendejo!*" Mya yelled as he ran toward Old Town Square's pedestrian-only plaza, quickly disappearing in a sea of nighttime entertainment seekers, his chortling buddies close on his heels. "*Mierda! Que un pinche idiota!*" She looked back at the faces that were peering around Catwalk's front door. "Go back inside, show's over!" She sighed when the door finally closed. She turned to find Jack much closer than before. His eyes were on her neck, and *just like that* her breath stalled. She rubbed at the goosebumps on her bare arms even though it was an eighty degree night. "Jack..."

He eased another step toward her, a muscle ticking in his cheek. Again, his cologne drifted over her, making her insides lush with memory.

He raised a hand to her neck and her head listed to the side, presenting itself shamelessly, even before his fingers made contact with her skin. One side of his lips quirked briefly before his gaze tracked back to her neck. He frowned. "You're bleeding." He seized her hand before she could touch it. "Don't. It could get infected by any number of pathogens your hands picked up in that cesspool."

"I'm fine," she murmured.

He dropped her hand and reached into his pocket, pulling out a small, red, zippered pouch. When he ripped open an antiseptic wipe packet, she giggled. "Of course you'd have a pocket first aid kit."

He ignored her, intent on cleaning, then applying antibiotic ointment and a band aid to a cut she couldn't even feel due to the super-charged emotions winging through her. Because of his closeness. His attention. She shivered. The man certainly knew how to focus.

When he'd finished ministering to her neck, neither of them spoke. The streets in this section of Old Town were always busy, but tonight, people were everywhere. Still, she couldn't concentrate on anything but him. His gaze moved up from her neck to snag on her lips. She watched his light blue-gray eyes go dark, her heart clutching, then releasing so forcefully it startled her. She couldn't draw a full breath, her chest vised by his magnetism. Her hands wanted to roam that solid chest, slide down his flat ab-tastic belly, and untuck his very practical hiking shirt from his very simple blue jeans and freaking *Go. To. Town.*

Breasts heavy, body tingly, she wrapped a hand around her hair and pulled the messy black mass to one side. *Will not take no for an answer tonight.* But the stubborn set of his chin and compressed lips made the let's-go-back-to-grandmas-and-screw-like-animals approach unfeasible, so....

"Let's go back inside and have a drink."

He didn't reply for the longest time, but pulled her to him abruptly when a group of drunken revelers stumbled by, then immediately set her an arm's length away again when they passed.

"...so you can torture me some more?"

"What?" He'd said something. Holy buckets, he smelled *gooooood*.

Felt even better.

Her eyes focused on the buttons of his shirt. Eight of them. Wouldn't take long to open that yummy package.

He grabbed her upper arms, bending down to replace the view of his buttons with his gorgeous eyes.

"Your buttons are a mad temptation," she said, forestalling anything he'd planned to say. His eyebrows pulled down sharply. He was so sexy when he was irritated.

"Are you inebriated?" Not waiting for her answer, he began pulling her down the street. She could see the new black truck he'd bought yesterday parked half a block away.

She giggled, knowing that she was most definitely not drunk—she'd only had one drink since she'd arrived at Catwalk— but her professor had said *inebriated*. "Have I ever told you I love your brain?"

"Let's go, Mya. Time for bed."

"Oh, hell, we finally agree!" She started running to his truck, but stopped suddenly and turned to him. "Wait! I can't leave Jazz."

Forty minutes and sixty-nine naughty fantasies later, she and Jack had Jasmine dropped off at her apartment and were pulling into Rosie's garage. Mya's skin vibrated all along her left side where she'd been pressed up against Jack while Jazzy had rode shotgun with them. Mya had reluctantly scooted over after they'd dropped her off, but the tension in the truck during the ride back home had been over the top. Now, they were both sitting in the truck, the garage door already shut, but neither one of them seemed to want to be the first to move.

When she opened her mouth to speak, Jack opened his

door, got out, slammed the door, and walked into Rosie's without a backwards glance.

Are you kidding me? Mya scrambled out of the truck and raced inside, blood pumping hard like she was being dumped off on the frontlines of a war. He was already in the only bathroom in the house. She pounded on the door so hard it rattled the pictures on the hallway wall. "We've got to get a few things ironed out, Whiteside. This is driving me crazy! You hear me in there? First you're all hot, alpha he-man protecting the little woman from big bad wolves, then you're so goddamn cold I'm getting frostbite and whiplash simultaneously. Why are you doing this?"

He whipped the door open, and *Oh. My. God.*

He was shirtless.

And the top button of his jeans was *undone*.

Her lips parted. Her thoughts scattered.

He groaned, railroading her back against the opposite wall with his whole frame. "Fuck, Mya, when you look at me like that..."

His hands framed her jaw, tilting her head back to receive his open mouthed kiss. His lower body leaned into her, stance widening, pinning her against the wall. She was ready. Her arms came around him, her hands grasping at his warm skin, the robust muscles of his back, pulling him closer, tighter against her.

His mouth skated down the side of her face, his stubble prickling, so raw and honest. Made her feel *alive*. He always did that. *How?* He leaned down further, raked her bra straps down her arms. Whispered something at the juncture of her neck and clavicle. At the upper swell of her breasts. Goosebumps ran circles around her arms. She pressed his dark head closer, raking her nails lightly, then harder across the broad flare of his shoulders. One of his legs slid between hers. He straightened, bringing his thigh in contact with her center. Pressing. Watching with hungry eyes as she shifted to fit against him better. Watching her as her lips parted on a swelling moan.

His eyes glittering in the shadows until once more his mouth slanted across hers in a claiming she'd never known.

Her body tightened, her hips grinding against his leg. She was so...*so*—

Cool air. Shoulders suddenly in a painful grip, pinned against the wall so her lower body wouldn't sag at the loss of his support. She opened her eyes. A savage look on Jack's face, his chest pumping, his hair wild, so very loved by her hands.

She tried to put a finger to his lips. *Don't speak. Please Jack.* Things always fell apart with words.

He pushed her fingers away, his eyes sharp with anger and something else that made her throat ache. "We're only good at this part, aren't we? I won't do this again. I *can't.* Don't you see? *God, Mya.*"

His hands released her, and his long legs put space between them until he'd reentered the garage. As his truck roared off into the night she slid down the wall in his grandmother's house, her tears trickling onto the beat-up oak floor where she'd first fallen in love with the boy who knew how to mine the secrets of her heart more effortlessly than the layers of earth that so fascinated him.

TEN

A blinding shaft of sunlight seared Jack's eyes when they snapped open. He hissed and shot up, banging his head on the swing-arm lamp hanging over the ancient sofa in the corner of his office. He swore foully as the polite knocking on his door continued. Couldn't be Mya because there was no such thing as a locked door to her. She would have either sweet-talked a maintenance man to unlock it for her, or more likely, would have picked the lock herself by now.

He swung his legs to the edge of the navy blue plaid sofa and reached for his glasses. "Coming. I'm coming," he muttered, glancing at his watch, then blanching at the time. *Nine-forty-nine.* He couldn't remember the last time he'd slept so late.

Couldn't be because he'd been up half the night with a raging hard on, berating himself for walking away from Mya's passionate embrace, now could it? His head pounded, but that was apropos with his relentless dick. Might as well have a matching set.

He rubbed his eyes, stretched his arms to the ceiling,

then opened his office door. Short and choppy black hair, black winging brows, green eyes heavily outlined with black pencil, and a narrow nose on a young lady who looked no older than a high school sophomore. She wore a red flannel shirt, a large black backpack slung over one shoulder. He'd never seen her before. "Can I help you?"

A full-on smile curved her lips, scrunching her eyes and making her seem much older somehow. "Sorry to bother you, Dr. Whiteside. I'm Timber Hollows," she extended a hand, "second year graduate geosciences fellow studying under Dr. Erickson. I've followed your work since your presentation on the confluence of lines along the frankincense trade route in the Arabian Desert that led to the discovery of the lost city of Ubar. And let me just say, wow, I was floored! You and Dr. Erickson are rockstars in the field, and I can't believe you're *both* here now."

"That's flattering, thank you. I look forward to reviewing your projects this coming semester." He smiled slightly, waiting to see if there was another reason she was stopping by on a July weekend morning when the rest of the campus was silent as a stone. She continued to stare at him for a moment, then seemed to recall herself. "So anyway, I pulled an all-nighter in Dr. Erickson's lab, and I saw you come in last night. I was getting ready to head out, and thought I'd stop by to introduce myself if you were still here."

Lilith hadn't mentioned any time-sensitive project that required working all night. But then, what did he know about academia anymore? He'd been out in the field for so long, he wondered briefly if he was making a mistake coming back to teach.

In more ways than one.

"Well, it's nice to meet someone so committed to the

cause. Now, go get some sleep. I'm sure I don't need to tell you how exacting Dr. Erickson is." He stepped back, intending to close the door, but Timber put her hand up.

"No kidding. Uh, she mentioned that a woman might show up around here from time to time. Something about needing protection because of an ongoing police investigation? Do you want me to keep our office open to her as well? I would have asked Dr. E, but I got the feeling she didn't want to talk about it anymore."

Odd. He'd never told Lilith why Mya was staying at Rosie's, and she'd never asked. It was nobody's business. Certainly not Lilith's, much less a graduate student's. "Why would she tell you that?"

"I don't know, really. Maybe because we're all pretty tight up here, and she didn't want me to be concerned if I saw a stranger walking around here after hours?"

Made sense. "Her name is Mya, and there's no need to concern yourself. I can assure you, she'll only be here under duress. She pretty much..." *Hates me—especially after how I left her last night—* "does what she wants to do. And that doesn't include twiddling her thumbs in any science department."

His cell phone rang on the small table beside the sofa. Timber gave him a thumbs-up sign, then waved and walked away. He didn't know what to make of Lilith sharing his living arrangements with her student. How many others had she told? This gossip, or lack of privacy, or whatever it was, was definitely one of the drawbacks of working inside a university research facility instead of the open air, where everyone pretty much left each other alone except to share their data.

He walked to his phone and picked it up, not recognizing the number. Five minutes later he hung up, his nerves taut, his pulse beating in his neck as he locked up his office and ran down the hallway.

He hurried to his truck, thinking about the call from Officer Ramos who'd reached out because the police department had been unable to contact Mya. Where the hell was she? He tried her number, swearing out loud when it went to voicemail.

According to Ramos, three days ago, the remediation crew cleaning Mya's HVAC system had found a nearly empty packet of matches advertising a local extended-stay hotel. Not sure if the police had missed it in their original sweep of Mya's house, they'd turned it over to the FCPD. Over the last couple of days, Ramos and his partner had done room-by-room wellness checks at the hotel, speaking to both guests and staff. When one of the housekeepers said she'd been repeatedly turned away from one of the rooms and another admitted finding a small, silver canister beside one of the guest washers that she later threw away, the police had secured a warrant. In the suspicious room, they found a folder containing pictures of Mya taken with a zoom-lens camera, a spreadsheet laying out her weekly schedule, and printouts of homemade bomb instructions.

Bombs.

Someone was stalking her with the intent to hurt her.

The thought of it made him want to rip someone apart and dig a grave so deep in the earth, the body would never be found.

He'd know how to do it, too.

He ground his teeth as he drove. He felt trapped. Trapped by his messed up feelings for her. Trapped by the compulsive need to protect her, the gut-wrenching desire to hurt anybody who even contemplated hurting her. Trapped by how out of control she made him feel. She made him crazy and unorganized and emotional. He hated that.

Feared it.

By the time he skidded into Rosie's driveway, he felt like a caveman, incapable of intelligent thought. Operating on emotion. Instinct.

The garage door leading into the mudroom banged against the wall as he charged into the house. "Mya!" He ran through the kitchen, down the hall, grasping at the door jam of the bathroom, then Rosie's room, until finally, he came to his bedroom, and found her there, curled on her side on his bed, her hands tucked beneath her cheek. The sunlight filtered gauzily through the plantation shutters and softened the angles of her face that were so strongly animated while she was awake. She'd always slept like the dead. Like her body had no other choice but to completely shut down after exerting such fierce biological vibrancy during her waking hours.

He crossed the room and went to his knees beside the bed, his throat closing off, the dizzy relief that she was truly safe warring with despair over his complex, deeply layered feelings for her. "I don't want to love you," he whispered. Unable to stop himself, he reached out a hand to run his fingers across her hair—God, he'd always adored her hair—spilling across his pillow. Looking at her like this, her restless body for once quiet, he didn't understand how this thing between them could be so complicated.

He loved her. Always had, always would.

Knew, too, that her love for him was just as consuming. He saw it in her expressive eyes, felt it every time she'd touched him these last fourteen days.

And Rosie had said so. Gramma never lied.

But sometimes love wasn't enough, was it?

Love shouldn't have to be so hard. Except it wasn't like a mathematical equation or a scientific method that could be systematically figured out. Emotions were messy, and sex, a terrible, magnificent complication that tumbled two people even further down a rabbit hole.

He shouldn't go there with her.

Shouldn't.

He hadn't ever wanted anything more in his entire life.

"Fuck, fuck, fucking, *fuuuck.*"

He unlaced his boots slowly, watching the steady rise and fall of her chest, his head raging against his heart.

He set his boots by the chair. His trembling fingers rose to the buttons on his shirt. Still, the woman whose very essence was imprinted on his soul slept on, unaware of the epic battle he fought against her siren call.

His head was losing.

After he placed the shirt carefully, deliberately—just so —on the chair, he rose above her, staring down at her.

She had utterly ruined him.

Anguish backdrafted through him as he eased onto the bed and stretched out, facing her. She slept on, her pink lips slightly parted. He admired her ability to sleep so deeply, even while it worried him. Would she wake if there was ever a fire? He propped his head on his hand to study the curve of her cheek, the tiny bow of her upper lip, the graceful arc of her eyebrows she had religiously plucked from the angst-filled age of fifteen.

The slight purple tint under her lush fan of black eyelashes. Like colored sediment layers of the earth, that atypical hue told him a story, and he was sorry for it.

So sorry.

"I always leave, don't I? Leave when all you need is for me to stay," he breathed between them before closing the distance, flexing his fingers before sliding them down the beautiful lines of her body. Shoulder, tricep, waist, hip, thigh...

She woke when his palm cupped her ass to pull her toward his warmth. He felt her awareness rise even before her hand came up to make the skin on his chest ignite.

"Jack?" Her voice was thick with sleep and something more. Spent tears?

He couldn't speak.

He leaned over to press her back into the mattress, rubbing his lips across hers, his chest filling, filling, filling with air and wonder and the trembling edges of hope. She sighed and her body softened in surrender beneath him. He slid down her frame, mouth at her ear, sucking her lobe, tongue tasting the salt of her neck. His hands pulled at her shirt. He leaned up, supporting her body with one hand to remove the red satin, and then unfasten her bra, and there she lay, her nipples rosy and pinched, as delicate and impossibly erotic as he remembered.

Hunger rode him. He shook with it, but he slowed his hands. They kneaded her breasts, brought them to his mouth, into his mouth, never enough, until she squirmed and moaned and he drifted down, drunk on her, to her tight belly where he'd long imagined planting babies. A laughing household full of children he could take into fields with shovels and compasses and a picnic and a radio and his beautiful, dancing Mya...

"*Jack.*"

He slid her tight pants off her legs, replying to her plea by scraping his teeth against her pubic bone. She shook and it made him feel invincible. He removed her thong as her hands twisted in the coverlet. He scooted off the end of the bed, hooked his arms beneath her thighs and slid her and the entire bedding down to his open mouth.

The first taste of her made him groan, his lips vibrating against her flesh.

"Oh. Oh, *Jaaack*. That's...so...perfect."

I know, baby. I know.

He tongued her. Slow, broad strokes, the quaking of her muscles, the pebbling of her dusky skin better than any lottery, any professional accolade. He nuzzled her, the stubble on his cheeks and chin a wicked contrast to the exquisite softness of her groin. He rocked his face against her, sucked at her, licking, pulling, drawing, demanding, his hands, one crawling up her belly, one gripping her thigh.

Until she gave him what he craved.

Her release, her cries bouncing off the ceiling as her neck arched, head pressing back into the pillow, her hands reaching for him. He released her thigh, threading their fingers together as the storm broke across her body, the sun's rays painting gold strokes across her breasts, tipping her black hair with magic. He hung on every thread of her passion, staying with her, loving her with his mouth until she pushed up, came to her knees, chest flushed, breasts bouncing, fusing her breath with his.

And he was a man lost.

———

THERE WAS a great rushing in her ears. A fullness inside that soothed as well as excited. She framed Jackson's face with her hands, terrified this was all a dream. That she'd once again laid down on his bed after he'd fled, and was imagining all this.

But his haunting blue-gray eyes stared back at her, bloodshot and so naked with desire they stole her breath.

"You came back," she whispered.

"I was wrong to leave."

A man of few words. *My man.* She pressed her lips to the corners of his eyes, pressing her thumb into his mouth. He sucked at it, creating a deep urgency within her. Her mouth replaced her thumb, relearning the shape and texture of his tongue as her fingers traced the lines and contours of his chest. The rounding of his pectorals, the peaks of his nipples, the ridges of his abs, indentation of his belly button, and the spear of fine, dark hair that crept down into his jeans.

She made him stand as she scooted to the edge of the bed. Held his gaze as she unbuttoned his jeans, slid them down his legs, and freed his erection. She spread her knees, beckoning him closer toward the edge of the bed where she sat. Then she took him in her hands, pressing kisses along the yoke of his hips. His stance widened, his strong capable hands going to her hair as she closed her eyes and took him in her mouth. Wanted to give him what he'd given her. More than simple, primal pleasure...

The abdication of self that came full circle a thousandfold—a self-actualization—when they linked up on a shared wavelength.

His sac tightened, and he pulled back, grasping her under the arms to toss her back on the bed. His eyes darkened in that familiar way, watching her breasts jostle. He was past the point of leaving her now. She smiled and stretched languidly.

"Feeling cocky?" His voice was even deeper than normal as he reached for something from his jeans' pocket, then stood looking down at her, rolling a condom down his length.

"Oh, yes, *mi hombre hermoso*." She circled her nipples with her fingertips, then ran her hands down her belly, sliding her first and middle fingers across her labia, slick, so sensitized from his thorough loving that she gasped on contact, then gasped again as he landed full frontal on top of her. His thighs hiked her legs apart, his hips driving, rubbing his erection against her. She tried to keep up with his passionate assault, then just let go. Surrendered to wherever he wished to take her, take them both in this moment.

Don't think about afterwards. He would start to think soon enough, and it would fall apart again.

Her heels pressed into his glutes as he lifted his hips. Closed her eyes as a wave of fear spread through her.

"Mya."

Don't think.

"Look at me. *Mya*."

His body stilled. She could feel the effort it cost him. She opened her eyes, praying he was still with her. "Don't think. Please, Jack." Her eyes prickled. She wanted to hide but his eyes wouldn't let her, his body pulsing at her center. *I can't bear it if you leave me right now.*

"I love you, Mya."

Tears blurred her vision. He kissed them away as his body slowly filled hers. Their joining, aching, slow, infinitely tender. Sighs and whispers wrapped them up in the arcane mystery as their hips met, drew apart, over and over, a slow dance carrying them to the well of their deepest desire. Finding each other there, they wandered through the maze of darkness to set each other free.

She clutched Jack to her breast when the pleasure shattered through her in a motley rush of heat and cold.

As his body seized, she laid herself bare, her walls lowered for him to storm. Come what may, she was open.

She was open.

To forever.

Or complete destruction.

ELEVEN

J ack's consciousness rose when something soft and warm shifted beside him, a berries and coconut scent washing over him. He blinked against the bright sunlight streaming through the shutters, realizing where he was—Rosie's guest bedroom—then closed his eyes again, pulling Mya closer against his body, her ass fitting perfectly into his hip girdle.

"Jack? Mya?"

His eyes snapped opened at the insistent call coming down the hallway. *Ah, great. Gramma's home.*

Mya grumbled in her sleep, and he smiled, nuzzling into her hair despite the awkwardness of the situation. It was about to get weird in three, two—

"Jack! Are you home?" His door opened abruptly. "I saw a new truck in the gara—" Gramma's eyes widened momentarily before a cheeky smile lit up her face. He put a finger to his lips, hoping they wouldn't wake Mya yet, but—

"Oh shit!" Mya jerked up, pulling the coverlet across her breasts, a rapid blush flooding down her neck to spread across her chest. "Rosie, sorry, I...*crap*." She tried to scoot to the edge of the bed, but Jack hooked an arm around her belly and slid her back against him.

"She's been praying for this all along, so don't worry," he drawled.

Rosie turned away to start arranging the knick-knacks on his dresser. "Sorry to barge in on you this way, but I never anticipated...the middle of the day! *Fascinating*. Aaaanyway, I'm back and I had such a lovely time and that Ivy is such a wonderful individual, and her parents' place....*oy vey!*"

Jack suppressed a grin. "Gramma, you mind giving us a minute to get dressed?"

Rosie looked embarrassed for the first time. "Oh, certainly! I'll be in the kitchen. Feel like pancakes? You make love mid-day. Why not eat breakfast out of order, too, right? Okay, then, very good."

She closed the door, singing down the hallway to the kitchen. Jack chuckled as Mya groaned.

"Oh my God, we were caught in bed by *tu abuela!*" She lunged away from him before he could grab her this time. The sight of her lithe, toned body made him forget all about grandmothers, pancakes, and getting caught.

"Come here, Mya."

She threw him a fierce frown as she jumped up and down, pouring herself into her itty bitty jeans. "We're out of condoms, *hombre*. Plus, I'm not getting busy with you while Rosie's in the house. She probably thinks I'm a *puta*," she spat. More Spanish self-recriminations followed.

"Trust me, she's thrilled." His smile dropped away. "First thing we need to do, though, is look for your phone. No more distractions." He'd told her about the break in the case after the first time they'd made love, asking to see her phone since Officer Ramos hadn't been able to contact her.

Mya's head poked through the top of her tight, red t-shirt. "You're not complaining are you?"

"Of course not, but the police found defaced pictures of you, a spreadsheet of your comings and goings, and instructions for making a bomb in that hotel room."

"Why can't they determine who was staying there?"

"I'd imagine most criminals use aliases," he replied. Rosie's command to join her in the kitchen came from down the hall. "So where's your phone?"

"It's in my purse next to the fridge. Must be dead."

When she left the room, he took his time dressing, savoring the newness of their connection. He'd known what he was missing when he was so far away, but he always kept those thoughts—those emotions—locked down. Now, he tried not to over-think his confession.

He'd told her he loved her. She hadn't said it back. Not that he'd expected her to. Not that he'd expected it to come flying out of his mouth either for chrissakes.

He closed his eyes, then followed his nose to the kitchen where Rosie was heaping pancakes on a plate, and Mya was digging through her purse.

"It's got to be here..." She upended all the contents of her purse on the counter. "Huh. Maybe it fell out in your truck on the way back from Catwalk." She started toward the garage door.

"Mya, wait," Jack quickly followed her to his truck. "You can't go anywhere alone anymore."

She opened the driver's side door, then paused. He looked over her shoulder to see a small folded note on the seat. He reached around her to pick it up, a chill threading through him even before he read the words.

She will be the death of your dreams. Let her go before you give me no other choice.

TWELVE

Mya replayed the ominous words of the note over and over in her mind. *She will be the death of your dreams. Let her go before you give me no other choice.*

Someone didn't want them to be together. Why? Who was it?

Someone had tried to hurt her all along, and Artie had suffered because of her.

Wait. She spun to Jack. "This is about *you*." He didn't speak, but she could see he realized it, too. "Whoever it is, she—or he—doesn't want me to be with *you*. This person wants you for herself." She grabbed the note from Jack's hands, tore it in half, and tossed it to the concrete.

"Mya, no! It's evidence." He leaned down to pick up the pieces. A methodological expression unfolded across his features like it always did when he had a puzzle to solve. He and Rosie spoke in hushed voices by the door to the house, glancing at her from time to time as she stood next to the truck, trying to think.

The part that really hurt was someone thought she was incompatible with Jack's dreams. How many others thought the same? Did they see her as a ball and chain that would hold him down, hold him back? She never wanted that. She understood the importance of dreams. If someone ever told her to give up on her dreams, she'd put them in the rearview mirror.

She didn't ever want to be the end of Jack's dreams.

Rosie held her phone against her belly. "Come inside now, love."

Mya walked woodenly inside as Jack's gramma wrapped up her call.

"I just spoke to Ivy. I'm going back to Denver in an hour." Rosie looked at Jack, placing a hand over her heart. "I'm worried about you two. Why don't you go to San Francisco a week early? It'll make me feel better."

Jack's glower darkened. "You're playing the feeble-heart card now?"

"*Jackson*," Mya scolded.

Rosie didn't smile. "It's justified. Please. I love you both."

"It'll be tough to leave for the whole week with school starting so soon," he said.

"Tough to find yourself at the mercy of some obsessive sociopath, too," Rosie said.

Mya looked at Jack, expecting to feel a million miles away from him, but something in his eyes pulled her close instead of pushed her away. He hooked Rosie in his arms and scooped Mya in as well, hugging them both. "Okay. Let me call Lilith. If she doesn't murder me first, we'll be on our way to San Francisco this afternoon."

JACK KISSED MYA, their lips lingering even though

gramma still poked around in the kitchen. His hand gripped Mya's jaw, trying to pour comfort into her skin, trying to reassure himself he could protect her. She pulled back first, running the pad of her thumb over his lower lip. "Who's obsessing over you?"

"I can't imagine anyone doing such a thing." Honestly. He always kept to himself. He went out with colleagues from time to time, and he'd gone home with a stranger or two over the years, but he'd never led anyone to believe he was relationship material. "I've never let anyone in."

"That doesn't mean someone hasn't loved you from afar. Or what they think is love anyway," she said.

He shook his head, at a loss. He kissed her again, then held her in his arms briefly before going to his bedroom and dialing Lilith's office phone.

"Dr. Erickson's office."

"Who is this?" he asked.

"Timber Hollows, starving graduate student who needs all the extra hours I can rack up," she laughed briefly before continuing, "Is this Dr. Whiteside?"

"Yes, is Dr. Erickson available?"

"She ran down to Dr. Jorgerson's office, but she should be back shortly. Is there something I can do for you?"

Lil had struck gold with this one. "Do you have the department's meeting schedule for this week?"

"Yeah, you need me to send it to you?"

"Yes, thank you. Does it look like there's anything that I absolutely shouldn't miss?"

"If you need to split, it's all good. There's nothing this week I can't take care of for you. If you want to give me your number, I can let you know if something comes up or your approval is needed on anything. Otherwise, this week and the next are okay to be gone. The week after that, not so much."

"Excellent. I appreciate your help, Ms. Hollows."

"You got it. And call me Timber. Hey, here's Dr. Erickson. Talk soon!"

He could hear the two women talking in low tones as the phone was passed to Lilith. "Trying to steal my research assistant already, Whiteside?" Lil said without preamble.

"I'm leaving for California a week earlier than I'd planned. Just checking to see if there's anything critical I need to attend to first."

His statement was met with a silence thick with censure. He'd never had an argument with Dr. Erickson, and he hoped one wouldn't start now. Sharing personal details felt unnatural to him, but he realized he needed to give a little so she could understand. Telling her about the break in the investigation would probably gain him the go-ahead, but something held him back from sharing that intel. "The dance competition is a week out, and Mya thought it would be advantageous for us to head to California early to practice in the venue where the competition is being held."

"Because dancing on one floor is so vastly different from another? How lame, Jackson."

His hand tightened on the phone. "You're being remarkably insensitive, Lil."

"Here's the thing, Jackson. Did you come back for research or for dancing? You've clearly lost your focus. I'm disappointed."

"I don't see any reason why you or I can't do what we do and have other hobbies at the same time."

"I disagree, but this isn't even about an extracurricular activity, Jack. This is about someone else."

Heat spread through his veins. "How would you feel if

someone you loved was in danger?" The minute the words were out of his mouth he regretted them, but he wasn't sure why.

"It would be damned nice to know what it felt like to love someone that much," she said, then hung up.

THIRTEEN

J ack pulled Mya out of the dip as the last strains of the music faded. *Perfecto!* She clapped her hands and then launched into his arms, wrapping herself around him. "We're ready! I knew we could do this!"

As the week in San Francisco had progressed, she'd felt their bond strengthening. When they'd left Fort Collins she'd worried the opposite would be true. That Jack's psycho secret admirer would drive them apart, but somehow it had had the opposite effect. This week had been a dream, and they were closer than ever. It had been a welcome relief to leave all the drama behind and not worry about their loved ones. Yes, the problems would be waiting for them when they returned, but for now she wanted to focus on the competition. Their dancing was more in sync than ever.

She ran over to her duffel bag and pulled out her street shoes, then sat down to remove her dance pumps. He stalked toward her with a look that ravished her on the spot. She shivered and giggled. "Let's get tattoos!"

He paused, an adorable confusion passing over his features. "What?"

"I've wanted one for a long time, but I never knew what I wanted until this moment. Let's go!"

He took hold of her hands and pulled her up. She would have ran out the door but he held her in place and began pressing persuasive kisses against her temples, her cheekbones, the corners of her lips.

"And now you know?"

"W-what?" When his hands skimmed across her nipples like that she couldn't think.

He chuckled against her mouth. "Know what ink you want?"

"Yessss. *Mmmmm.*"

His hand, large and proficient, found its way under her kimono top, fingernails lightly scraping her sides, up, over her breasts, skimming the sensitized skin spilling above the demi bra she wore, then sliding to her back, pulling her hips tight against him.

"What would you have them draw?"

"Stop. T-talking," she ordered. His lips trailed across her neck, his breath raising goosebumps all across her body.

"I thought you liked it when I came out of my shell."

"I like your hands on *my* shell better right now."

"What else do you like?" His hands curled under her butt cheeks, lifting her body, spreading her legs, hooking them around his trunk. She wrapped her arms around his neck, licked the side of his face, and ground herself into the thick, hard ridge in his dress slacks, too far gone to feel any shame.

"Glad to be of service."

"*Mmmm.*"

"Looks like I'll have to be the sensible one again." His

stuffy words belied the rough-edge to his voice that portended all manner of carnal delights. He began walking to the back of the room.

She lifted her lips from his neck. "It's so late, no one will be coming."

"Oh, I disagree. More than one of us will be coming. Very, very loudly," he said wickedly, continuing across the dance floor. He set her on her feet in the janitor's closet, pulled the door shut, wrapping them in cozy darkness. Then her shirt was off, quickly followed by her bra, her pants, then he was on his knees and—*ooooo*—his clever fingers were soon replaced by his mouth and—

Oh. My. God.

A thin stream of light filtered from the crack beneath the door. Her vision blurred as she climaxed at the third sweep of his tongue. The orgasm unfurled down her legs. She grasped his shoulders, sinking into his arms as he stood, his mouth fusing to hers. Blindly, her fingers found the condom in his pocket. She pulled his erection free, sheathing him slowly as he groaned.

His forearm swept a menagerie of cleaning supplies off the tiny counter before he hoisted her upon it. They gasped in unison as their bodies met. He pulled back, fingers of one hand digging into the skin of her waist, the other hand palming her breast. He groaned and drove home again. And again. Over and over until the pleasure burst at her center and carried outward like bright, pulsing shrapnel that healed instead of destroyed.

He grasped her to him as his body spasmed. She wrapped her arms around his shoulders, holding him until the tremors evened out. *Tell me you love me.* He hadn't since that first time they'd made love a week ago. Of course, she hadn't said the words either. Had he really meant it, or was it simply the overwhelming release that caused the words to fall from his lips?

He kissed her once more in the dark, then reached back to switch on a single lightbulb that flickered in the small room while they cleaned up. They froze when someone entered the outer room where they'd left their things in the heat of the moment. Jack helped her finish dressing, then they ran out of the closet, grabbed their bags, and smiled their goodbyes to the surprised, grizzled man standing with a mop in his hand.

They ran out into the evening, laughing. "Ready for some ink?" he asked.

Mya glanced at him as he twined his fingers with hers. "Are you serious?" This wasn't like him. Two years ago he hadn't wanted her to get one. Tattoos weren't logical. They carried risk of infection, allergic reaction, and scarring, he'd argued. So she hadn't gotten one to appease him.

"If it makes you happy, I want to be there when you get it," he said, and she realized this wasn't the professor talking anymore. This was her perceptive Jack. The boy who'd rode his bike around three neighborhoods to gather enough stargazer lilies—*lilium orientalis,* according to his field guide —to fill two metal buckets which balanced on either end of his handlebars. She'd been sad, and he'd come to her door bearing a fragrant armload of her favorite flower.

How she'd missed that sweet, sensitive soul.

Two hours later, Mya wore a butterfly and *Carpe Diem* inked behind her ear. Jack had held her hand the whole time. *I'm here in this moment with you,* his gaze had told her, and she loved him more than ever. This time would be different. They'd both grown. They wanted each other and would overcome whatever obstacles stood in their way.

And they would kick ass at the competition tomorrow.

They wandered the busy streets, simply enjoying the humanity around them, appreciating being together because they knew now what it felt like to be without each other. They had no more secrets. Jack had told her he'd been in touch with the police this week, but there were no new developments. So now, this precious time together felt like a reprieve. Tomorrow night after their competition they'd head back to reality.

For one more night it would be just the two of them.

Mya squeezed his hand. "Take me back to the hotel."

He paused on the sidewalk, their bodies parting the stream of people who continued to flow around them. Seeing the look in her eyes, he hailed a cab and pulled her on his lap on the way to their hotel. They nearly made love in the elevator. He opened their room door, and they crashed into the wall, all open mouths and fingers grasping, pulling, insistent. He guided them to the bed, and she let go, ready to sink onto the mattress, but he yanked her back. She shook off her stupor when his attention shifted around them.

She blinked when he released her and turned on the light.

Their room was completely ransacked.

FOURTEEN

Jack rubbed his hands together, then ran them down his black dress slacks, visualizing the intricate dance steps he and Mya would perform in twenty minutes. He hadn't been this nervous when presenting his doctoral thesis, speaking at various United Nations events, or even standing before the greatest minds in his field at the Global Summit on Geosciences.

But this was about his woman's dream. He couldn't let her down.

He paced back and forth in front of the dressing room where Mya was putting the finishing touches on her outfit. If she wasn't out in five minutes, he was going in after her. Especially after what had happened last night.

Their hotel room had been destroyed, but nothing taken. Responding law enforcement said it looked like a revenge crime instead of a robbery. Their sociopathic stalker had found them in San Francisco. Which was discomfiting to say the least, but Mya had been surprisingly calm. Two years ago, he'd never have imagined how composed she could be, asking all sorts of reasonable questions of the officers. She had matured in many ways.

Afterwards, they'd transferred their belongings to another hotel and tried to get some sleep. He hadn't drifted off until the California sun began to peek under the heavy drapery of the room, but he'd held Mya all though the night, listening for subtle, unfamiliar noises that might mean trouble and running through a possible list of who might be behind these attacks.

Everyone in Mya's circle knew where this year's tango championship was being held. And anyone in his circle could easily find out. But who was it, and why?

Clapping and cheering boomed from the auditorium. Jack put his phone back in his bag and shoved it in one of the lockers. A man with slick-backed, blond hair pulled along a woman in a dress that dropped blue feathers as they sped by for their turn under the lights.

"Whiteside-Castillo, line up in ten, or you'll be passed over!" a woman with frizzy gray hair and a well-tailored, ivory pantsuit yelled his direction.

He gave her a thumbs up and turned back to the dressing room door. *Thirty more seconds, Mya—*

When the door swung open, his gaze fastened to her red-painted lips first, the bow of her upper lip so much more pronounced with its scarlet outline. Her dark hair was pulled back into a low bun adorned with fresh red roses. Black chandelier earrings cascaded extravagantly to her shoulders.

Bare shoulders. Beautiful, structural, soft.

He swallowed hard as his gaze tracked slowly across the line of black lace the formed the top border of her dress and hugged her upper biceps. Falling below the three-inch band of black lace, her mid-thigh dress bled into red. The contours of the dress hugged her body, caressing every line —slim as it rode across the plane of her belly, flaring slightly at her narrow hips, then curling in across her ass with a fall of black lace bustled behind her that would look amazing as she moved. Black, sparkling beads encircled her wrist, her fingernails a fire-engine red, while her legs—poetry in motion—were bare to her strappy, ebony heels.

He felt slightly drunk as his eyes took their time on the way back up. "You are a vision."

"Thank you for the flowers," she turned to the side to give him a better view of the roses in her hair.

"I would have brought you *lilium orientalis*, but the hue wouldn't have worked with your dress." His heart stuttered when her eyes grew misty.

"The roses are lovely, Jack. They will bring us good luck."

"We don't need luck. We'll simply do the best we can. And hope it's enough to get us in the top three."

She nodded, then extended her hand. "I have something for you as well."

He narrowed his eyes on the small gift box in her hand which he hadn't noticed on his earlier inspection. "When did you have time to get something? You'd better not have been out on your own."

Her eyes crinkled with a small smile. "I picked it up last week at home." She pushed the small package into his hands. He removed the red bow and unwrapped the plain white paper. A jewelry box. It made his heart start to thrum. He glanced up at her when she folded her hands in front of her body. "You should be saving for your studio."

She twisted her hands. "It's not much. Just open it."

"Whiteside-Castillo, two minutes or you might as well board a plane back home right now!" the stagehand barked.

"Coming!" Mya called back. "*Andale*, Jack!"

His heart was in his throat when he eased the jewelry box open. Two square, gold cufflinks sat upon white velvet, a textured globe etched in each square. The earth's continental detail was meticulous. He looked up at her. "I've never seen such a thing."

"You like them?" Her big hazel eyes were so hopeful.

"They're perfect." He plucked them from their velvet nest. "Put them on me."

"Whiteside-Castillo...*twenty seconds, nineteen...*"

Mya laughed and hauled him toward the line of other dancers waiting their turn. There were only two couples in front of them now. She took the cufflinks from his hands and threaded them through his shirt cuffs. Then she straightened his red suspenders and black bow tie and brushed some lint off his black suit coat. "There, you look positively dashing. If we had all women judges, we'd win for certain."

Those sassy dimples melted him every damn time. "Thank you, Mya." He leaned down to hug her, but she pushed him away with a nervous grin.

"You'll ruin the lipstick!" She winked at him, then put her hands up, indicating their opening stance. As they pseudo-moved through their first sequence, he watched the play of drama on her face.

"Mya, we need to talk..."

Her concentration faltered, her eyes carefully avoiding his. "Don't do this right now. Please, Jack. Keep your head in the game. That's the only way I can do it, too. Okay?"

"Okay."

And suddenly it was their turn.

His heart pounded as they walked onto the stage. Mya's pulse flickered like butterfly wings against his palm when they held hands. He squeezed her fingers, running his gaze over the two levels of overflowing balconies that would be watching their every move. The five judges were stationed on a raised platform on the western side of the dance floor. Three men and two women. Jack squeezed Mya's hand once more before they separated, got into position and looked down at the floor, waiting for their song to begin.

The space was unbelievably silent for such a large, packed venue. Jack could hear his own breathing. He inhaled deep and then exhaled as quietly as possible. The opening strains of the music drifted through the room, pushing against the bodies assembled, watching, judging, expert eyes ready to find every flaw in their performance.

Don't. Fail.

Salida. Enter the dance. He moved, slow, slow—*keep it slow*—fought the rush of his blood, his nerves. Slow and flow toward her. *Caminar.*

Then she was in his arms. They locked eyes. He looked, looked, *searched* as they moved into the first full sequence. *Barrida y arrastre.* A sweep and drag. Her feet sliding across the wood, her body following the slightest pressure of his fingers and heel of his palm against her lower back as he moved her into a twisting *enrosque* of a turn which she follow up with a perfectly executed *boleo*, her right leg whipping back.

He could hear applause, could feel the hundreds of eyes upon them, but all that mattered was Mya. Her face keenly translating the emotion of the song that they'd chosen together. The music, so complex, reflective of all the layers they brought to their relationship. The depths and the heights.

A *freno* and a *gancho*, her hook so flawless as it moved

into multiple *ochos*. Back and forth, back and forth. Strong. Passionate.

So completely Mya. The tango could have been made for her.

She felt good—*so good*—in his arms. He could dance like this with her forever. Their feet sandwiched. *Mordida.* Their eyes held as the song paused. An expectation. A waiting, trembling on the edge of something too big for words.

The music shifted into the bridge, and they broke into *la corrida*, rhythmically walking double time across the floor's expanse. *Almost to the finish.*

The song segued back into the melody. They performed some of the flashier moves again. The crowd cheered loudly. Mya didn't seem to notice, so caught up in the story of the song. He guided her into *la cruzada*, the cross, then picked her up and held her immobile against his chest, her legs split, a gazelle caught midstride.

He turned her in his hold, noses, lips, chins on point, close, so close, an ache, a massive temptation not given into. The audience felt the temptation, holding their collective breath as Mya slid inch by tortuous inch down, down, down the front of his body until her feet were once again planted on the ground. Her heart slugged against his chest, insistent, and he couldn't hold it in any longer.

"I love you," he whispered, then pushed her out into the beginning of the final sequence. Her eyes widened, painted lips falling open as she faltered. Her *sacada* more than a displacement. He pulled her back into the embrace, using the pressure of his hands more strongly than usual until she found her groove again. And not a moment too soon. He pushed her out, waited for her eyes on him signaling she was ready, then they went in for the lift. She slid across his left shoulder, he pulled her around to his right, then set her back on her feet so she could draw a circle on the floor with her foot. A perfectly executed *lapiz*. He drew her up roughly, their hands scraping up each others cheeks into their hair...

And the dance ended.

They remained in that position for long seconds, their chests rising and falling rapidly with the physicality of the dance. The drama of the story played out in the song, and between them.

She pulled away first with a show-stopping smile. They faced the cheering crowd and bowed once, then twice as the audience continued its raucous applause. Then they linked hands and moved off stage. He looked at her, wishing, praying she'd look at him. Hoping against hope that his moment of weakness on the floor just now—his words from the heart—would have the desired effect. But the vibe was wrong somehow.

When they made it backstage, she broke away from him, running for the dressing room, and his heart bottomed out.

FIFTEEN

M ya bolted for the bathroom, too overcome with all these big feelings to trust herself to turn around and tell Jack she. Had. To. Go. *Now.* Hopefully he remembered that nerves always hit her worse after-the-fact. She'd always been like this. Like her psyche refused to acknowledge how important something was until it was over.

Inside the stall, she whipped her dress up, sat down, and chewed on her fingernails, her fingers quaking, her heart racing even faster than when they'd initially stepped on the dance floor. A giddy smile was starting to make her cheeks ache.

It was over and out of their hands now. It was up to the judges.

We killed *it.*

And Jack loves me.

She clapped her hands, pumped a fist in the air, and giggled like a naughty kindergartner who'd pulled one over on her babysitter. The two women who'd been deep in conversation by the sanitary napkin station stopped talking suddenly. "Don't mind me in here. Sorry, just nervy, I guess," she called. Then she flushed the toilet and put herself back together as someone pounded on the stall door.

"*Mya*. You okay in there? Talk to me."

"Jack?" She exited the stall, unable to restrain a toothy smile when he blushed and offered a very staid apology to the two glaring women who called him a pervert as they stormed out of the ladies' room.

Mya pushed by him, grasping the edges of the door, every Spanish word that issued from her mouth releasing a little more of her tension. "You're just jealous you don't have anyone willing to brave the ladies' bathroom for you!" She turned back to find Jack looking adorably perplexed. "There, I feel *so* much better. Confrontation is so cathartic!" She flew at him, and—as she knew he would—he caught her.

"Mya, what the actual fuck?"

She leaned back in his arms and rained kisses all over his face. "Don't you remember how touchy my belly gets after big stuff?"

"*Ah*." His face and shoulders relaxed. "You scared me. I thought..."

She silenced him with a kiss. She knew what he was thinking. That he'd told her he loved her, and she was rejecting him. She poured herself into the kiss to make him feel the depth of her love for him. Her passion, her hope for their future. Her fingers combed through the silk of his hair, holding him as tightly as he held her. Their breaths became shorter, harder, their fingers more daring. He walked with her in his arms until her back braced against the far wall, then leaned his body so firmly against her he didn't need to use his hands to support her.

Which left them free for other pleasurable pursuits. He

drove his hips into the cradle of her pelvis. She broke contact with his mouth to release the pent up tension in a deep moan that reverberated the entire length of her throat.

"Oh, I like that sound, Mya." Again with his strong hips.

She was coiling, ready to spring but a loud gasp over Jack's shoulder shook her from her stupor.

"I'm calling security!" a woman with large round sunglasses and a beret wailed.

Jack set Mya down, placing his body in front of her, but Mya grabbed his hand and pulled him along as she raced, laughing, from the room while he dropped apologies as they fled. Everyone stared, but she didn't stop running until they'd exited the auditorium to stand in the balmy California sunshine.

On the sidewalk outside the venue, Mya leaned over, hands on her knees to catch her breath. "This day keeps getting better and better," she said. "Maybe we should stay a little longer than we planned. We've never taken a vacation together, do you realize that?"

He rubbed her back, then her shoulders as she stood. The warmth and amusement in his eyes made her body go lax and shivery all over again.

"I *do* realize. Something I hope we can remedy very soon, but first, we need to get inside. They should be announcing the winners soon."

"Right. Okay," she exhaled, her belly turning over again. The last three weeks had been a whirlwind, but some of the best days of her life. All because of Jack.

He loves me.

She took his hand, squeezing, and they walked inside.

Now if they could just place in the top three, all her dreams would be on their way to coming true.

SIXTEEN

The energy in the ballroom cranked higher when the emcee stepped into the spotlight. Jack raised his eyes to the two stories of balconies overlooking the dance floor. People crammed together, jockeying for the best spot to watch the next couple be crowned Argentine Tango USA champions. His fingers laced with Mya's as she did one her appealing little nervous dances. He squeezed her hand and she looked up, her eyes wide, happy, and full of promise. A lump settled in his throat. "I hope I was good enough to get you a placement."

She took his hand in both of hers. "Are you kidding? You were amazing. Thank you for saying yes on such short notice. I know I'm not easy to be around all the time." When he raised an eyebrow, she nudged him with a mock-glare before continuing, "but I know you're too much of a gentleman to agree with me. So, *anyway,* even if we don't place, I'll always be grateful that you tried to help."

He leaned down to kiss her, his eyes closing on contact with her lips. And like always, his body recognized her. He turned toward her, ready to deepen this connection, and everyone else be damned, but she smiled against his lips and pulled back. "They're announcing third place," she whispered.

The couple named as the third place winners emerged from the back of the shadows into the spotlight to claim their trophy. Jack's pulse stroked his neck. Two chances left for Mya's sponsor to back her...

"And our runner-up couple hail from the Rocky Mountain state of Colorado. Please everyone, put your hands together for the dance team of Mya Castillo and Jackson Whiteside..."

A small squeal leaked out of her mouth before she slammed it shut, looking dignified and elegant as they walked toward the judges. Jack smiled at the cameras snapping from the darkness and accepted the trophy, wishing he had both hands on the woman he loved. Hers were occupied with an enormous bouquet of flowers.

Sixty minutes later, they'd changed and departed the auditorium. Jack's heart was full, listening to Mya's endless chatter about the studio she'd soon get to open, the students she could reach, the pure joy in her voice the only reward he'd ever need. They walked down the boulevard, hand in hand, Jack pulling their two suitcases behind him, neither of them quite ready to head to the airport for their return flight home.

Could anything be this perfect? Sure, Mya still befuddled him at times, but she kept him on his toes. Kept life interesting with her passion. When someone loved as hard as she did, was it even fair to wish she wouldn't fight or get upset in equal measure? She was a woman of extremes, mostly on the positive end of the continuum. He'd been around many women who kept their feelings tightly reined, but that was much more exhausting to deal with because he never knew where he stood with them. Their mouths said one thing, but their eyes and actions contradicted every damn thing.

He'd take Mya's emotions on her sleeve any day. Action that matched emotion was logical. What he could see, he could deal with.

"...call it *La Buena Vida*?" She paused, smiling, a small, confused furrow to her brows when he continued to remain silent. "Jack? Do you like the name?"

He had no idea what she'd said, but whatever it was, she only wanted him to agree anyway. "I love it."

Her eyes twinkled. He'd been caught in his duplicity, but both of them were too elated to take issue with it. "We have time for a quick bite to eat before we catch a cab to the airport, right?" she asked.

He nodded, then let her lead the way to the nearest restaurant with outdoor seating as he fished his ringing phone out of his bag. Mya had made all the calls to their family afterwards, so he hadn't even bothered with his phone. When he pulled it out of the suitcase pocket however, he saw that he'd missed no less than five calls. All from Lilith.

Who was currently calling again.

His stomach tightened. Lil wasn't one to waste time on frivolous phone calls. If she'd tried to reach him this many times, it was something significant. "Hello Lilith."

"Have you listened to my voicemails? I've been trying to reach you for three hours. Maybe more."

"We were compet—"

"They found *more*, Jack."

More evidence of Mya's stalker was his first thought, but he hadn't discussed the case in much detail with Dr. Erickson. "More what?"

"*Scrolls*, Jack. More Dead Sea Scrolls. We're talking a cache of about a hundred, maybe more. *God*. We have to go back as soon as possible!"

Whoa. His breath stalled in his chest. Mya came around the corner holding up a reservation ticket like it was trophy in itself, her smile sliding from her lips when she discerned the look on his face. He swallowed hard.

"...are you hearing me, Jackson? This excavation will cement our contributions for the rest of our careers. These new ones are located in a cave *east* of the Dead Sea. Who knows how many more there actually are? More books of the Bible might be found on these scrolls. It's truly historic. When are you getting back? Forget that, just change your ticket at the airport and meet me in Jerusalem within the next forty-eight hours. We'll figure out how to get to Jordan from there."

His mouth was dry. This couldn't be real. "What about CSU?"

"After overseeing this excavation, we'll be able to name our university anywhere in the world. I don't know why you're wasting time asking all these ridiculous questions. All you need to know is, this project will change your life in untold, thrilling ways. See you in Israel, Jack."

Lilith hung up. She assumed everything. Assumed he'd jump at the chance. Who wouldn't? This was a find of a lifetime for a geoarchaeologist.

But to reach the pinnacle of his career, he'd have to leave the woman he loved. Again.

SEVENTEEN

Mya parked in her single car garage and entered her kitchen, the late hour of the night making the familiar turquoise paint as murky and full of shadows as her soul. As much as she loved Rosie's house, she had missed her own place. She left the lights off, dropped her purse on the counter, and flopped into a chair at the table, too exhausted to even make it into the living room. She put her elbows on the table, her head in her hands, and released a shuddering sigh. The backs of her eyes prickled, and she let the tears come because she was finally alone.

She'd spent the last hour with Aspire Athletic, planning out the new studio's details, sketching out the initial blueprints, outlining her dream come true. The process should have filled her with joy. Yet now, she was shattered by the knowledge that she was losing Jack when she thought he'd truly be hers forever.

Things had been so tense between them during the two days they'd been home from San Francisco. She'd known—she'd just *known*—their peaceful bubble had popped when she saw his face while he talked to Dr. Erickson.

Damn the woman!

She didn't blame Jack for being unsure what he was going to do. This was the excavation of a lifetime. But what about their love? That was forever, too...

But I haven't told him!

She lifted her head from her palms. Her pulse started pounding in her throat. How could she have *not* told him? Her love had been fighting to break free and spew all over him since he'd walked back into her life three weeks ago. Ah, hell, it had never died. He'd told her he loved her over and over the last couple of days. And she hadn't once said it back!

She jumped out of her seat and took two steps, flicking on the light by the sink, her eyes falling on a note in Jack's neat handwriting on the counter.

Meet me at the entrance to Horsetooth Reservoir at ten thirty. We have to talk.

Butterflies erupted in her belly. Horsetooth at night was a place for romance. A local group had held fundraisers to purchase hundreds of outdoor light strings to festoon the first leg of the hike up Horsetooth Mountain. It was dreamy. Yet the way the note ended, it didn't sound like he was in the mood for romance.

Then again, he'd entered her home, so he wasn't trying to avoid her, so...

Ugh. This was either going to be the best or worst night of her life.

She glanced at the clock on the wall. She had twenty minutes to meet him. She turned, gasping to see a moving shadow in the hallway. She scrambled for a knife from the butcher block. A figure emerged in the kitchen. A young woman, twenty-something and goth, with pixie-short, black hair and heavy-handed rims of black eyeliner on a cool, green gaze. She raised her hands in a universal no-harm, no-foul motion. "Sorry to scare you. Please, put the knife down. I'm Timber, a graduate fellow in the Geosciences Department of CSU. I work with Dr. Erickson and Dr. Whiteside."

Mya's heart hammered forcefully. She lowered the knife, but didn't release it. "What are you doing inside my house?" Had she set off the tear gas? Mya wracked her brain trying to remember if Jack had mentioned any graduate students.

Timber smiled patiently. "Jack's been sleeping here since you came back from San Francisco. I was hoping to speak to him, but apparently I just missed him." She inclined her head to Jack's note on the counter. "Unfortunately, I'll have to do things another way."

A trickle of sweat slid down the center of Mya's back. "Jack isn't here, so you should leave before I call the police."

Timber took a step toward her like she wasn't even fazed that Mya clutched a nine-inch butcher knife in her right hand. "I tried to tell Jack that you'd be the death of his dreams. I tried to tell him in so many ways. He thinks he's going to propose to you tonight, but I won't let him throw away everything he's worked so hard to achieve."

She paused six feet away, smiling, and it all came together for Mya.

You'll be the death of his dreams.

"You put the note in his truck." Which also meant she was responsible for the tear gas. Mya lunged for her phone laying on the table, but Timber pulled a handgun from her waistband and slammed it against Mya's forehead. Mya went down in a white-hot flash of pain. Blood dripped on the floor next to her hands as she stared down, trying to stop the room from spinning. Timber kicked the knife across the room, then pressed the barrel of the gun at the base of Mya's skull.

Mya blinked down at her kitchen tile, nauseous, the room winking in and out in black. "Please don't do this. Jack is a good man. He deserves to be happy."

"And you think you're the one who can do that? Sure didn't work the last time, did it?"

Tears began to mingle with blood dripping down onto Mya's hands. "People change."

Timber laughed. "If I believed that, I would have gone back to my abuser daddy when he offered me a larger trust fund. But everybody lies, especially when they tell you they've changed. No more talking, get up!"

There could be no good ending to this kind of story. She'd have to fight, or become another statistic. She couldn't let Jack or her family live through that.

She'd just have to wait for the right moment and pray she got it right.

EIGHTEEN

J ack tried not to look at his watch one more time. *Chlorofluorocarbons, cinder cone, concretion, contact metamorphism...* He exhaled heavily and kicked at the gravel along the light-strewn path, wondering if he should've made his note less ambiguous. A solitary owl hooted across the valley, its loneliness an omen of what he'd have to look forward to if he didn't get this right.

He'd already been waiting an hour for Mya. An hour past the time he'd asked her to meet him. Was this supposed to be her answer?

He was going to pass on the second excavation.

He should have waited at her house, then told her, then brought her out here. What if he'd made a mistake by not telling her right away? Maybe she interpreted his note as the precursor to letting her down easy.

Fuck.

He knew she was working late, then meeting with her sponsor, but what was keeping her? Their interactions had been exceedingly strained the last couple of days. He understood her withdrawal. All the baggage she carried from losing her father, and then of course, her mother's disease had robbed their family of another parent's leadership. So yes, he understood that she needed to put some distance between them while he made his decision. She'd told him she wouldn't blame him if he seized the opportunity.

She'd even told him she would wait. That had blown him away. She was still crazy, passionate, unpredictable Mya, but she'd grown up. When the chips fell, she was on his side.

He pulled the plane ticket to Israel out of his pocket, anxious to watch her face while he ripped it up. He knew now without a doubt that he wanted to build a family with her—build forever with her—more than he wanted to spend countless hours in a desert examining inanimate objects and sediment that would have no lasting impact on his life beyond professional honors.

"Where are you, Mya?" He gazed at the stars twinkling above the lights, above the swooping bats. She'd love it out here. It was a warm night. A few couples snuggled on benches that dotted the first section of the path, the mood soft and languid. He turned to look toward the parking lot. Cars were exiting, none entering. His heart ached. Self doubt crept in like a January wind slipping through a broken window seal.

He carefully folded his airline ticket, put it in his pocket, and walked to his truck. He kept the music off as he drove back to Mya's. He didn't want to hear any slow songs. They would manipulate his hormones, a neuroscientific cause-and-effect that would make everything harder.

Her house was dark when he pulled into her driveway. *Please be sleeping.* She'd been driving so hard. And with all their practicing for the competition—along with their inability to keep their hands off each other—they hadn't slept enough the last few weeks. He took one last deep breath before he used the key to get inside. In the kitchen, her purse was on the counter, as well as her phone, and on the floor...his note.

And what looked to be watery smears of blood.

"Mya!" He ran through the house, flicking on all the lights. With each footfall, each room unoccupied, his anxiety ratcheted higher. He sprinted into the garage. Her car was gone, so she wasn't next door at Rosie's. Where had she gone? *Think logically. Don't assume the worst.* There were no signs of struggle.

Yeah, but that fucking blood.

She could've gotten a bloody nose. It was notoriously dry this time of year.

It wouldn't be that aqueous, though.

Besides, where the hell was she?

Kidnapped. The word shot around his mind faster and faster making him nearly lightheaded with panic and anger. He pulled out his cell phone, checking in with Rosie, Cole, Ivy, Natalia, Andre, and Jasmine.

No one had heard from Mya.

Something's really wrong. She would've told *someone* what she was up to. He started toward the door. He'd check at her studio, and then track down her sponsor. If they were dead ends, his next call would be Officer Ramos. His phone rang as he slid into his truck. His pulse surged, but it was only Timber. "You're wasting your youth by spending it exclusively in the office, Timber. You should be out partying with your cohorts." The line was silent for a heartbeat, and it felt wrong. He'd never been so unprofessional with graduate students before. "My apologies. I'm not myself tonight. Can we talk tomorrow?"

"Oh, it's nothing major," she assured him. "I thought I'd just mention that Mya had stopped by the office a bit ago."

Thank God. He slumped back against his truck seat and ran a hand down his stubbled cheek. "Is she still there?"

"No, sorry, it was really awkward. She threw the trophy you guys won through the glass door, screaming that you can keep it because all you care about is accolades. She said she hopes you go to Israel and never come back."

Jackson's gut free-fell into nothingness. He tried to swallow, but his throat was dry. "Are you sure? That doesn't sound like her," he managed in a hoarse voice.

"It doesn't? I thought it was remarkably in character. I'm really sorry, Mr. Whiteside. I know you like her, but I think you're probably better off without so much drama in your life. But of course, that's for you to decide."

He didn't know what to think. The scene probably explained why she didn't have her purse. Sounded like she'd read his note and went ballistic. Just left the house in a rage, taking the one thing that represented what they'd worked so hard to achieve. The thing that he'd thought brought them back together.

His whole life stretched before him, as barren as the desert he'd probably retreat to. "Did she say where she was going?"

"No. She came, exploded, then took off. I hope she makes it home alright. She seemed...*unhinged.* By the way, Dr. Erickson sprang for a ticket for me, too, so I'll meet you at the airport in a—"

Jack didn't hear the rest of what Timber said before he hung up. He and Mya had been here before. But this time felt even worse. His hopes had been so high, so strong. And the higher you flew, the harder you fell.

He removed the ticket from his pocket again, hating it,

but knowing he couldn't stay in Fort Collins knowing everything he really wanted was within arm's reach, but not his to have and hold.

The red-eye flight to Israel departed in three hours.

Jack stared at Mya's dark house one last time, then turned off his engine, slipped out of his truck, and went to wake Rosie to say goodbye.

MYA WOKE IN THE DARK, a dank, musty odor filling her nostrils. She was on her side, hands and feet zip tied. Her forehead pulsed and burned where Timber had cuffed her with the gun. *This can't be happening.* She had no concept of time or place, other than it must still be nighttime, and she must be somewhere below-ground if the stagnant, mildew scent was any indication.

She had to get free before Jack's flight departed. She couldn't bear it if he thought she didn't love him.

Please believe in me. In our love.

Had she given him enough reason to, though? She'd always been the one to test his love.

She gasped at the pain in her head, not wanting to cry out in case Timber was somewhere close. She finessed herself into a sitting position, then used her abdominal muscles to raise her legs, then exerted her thigh muscles apart as she forcefully dropped her heels. The plastic zip ties busted on the third try. She waited a moment for the worst of the stabbing in her head to pass, then scooted on her butt until she bumped into something solid to push herself up into a standing position. She took a deep breath, then raised her hands overhead, then drove them down rapidly, using her belly as the strike force as she jerked her hands apart. The zip ties broke apart like when she'd practiced last spring at her brother's insistence. *Thank you for your anal safety demands, Cole.*

She panned out with her hands in front of her as she carefully made her way toward the sliver of light well above her line of sight. Her feet bumped into something solid. Stairs, narrow and sliver-ridden. She was in a basement, then. Was Timber still here? She obviously wanted her out of the way. Why hadn't she killed her already?

The violent creaking of the stairs made the hairs rise on the back of Mya's neck. She tried the door handle and found it surprisingly unlocked. Her breath whooshed out in relief until she opened the door and a bucket dumped brown-gold liquid into the barren, ramshackle room and all over her. *Gasoline!* It soaked her hair and clothes, the overpowering scent burning her nose, the hydrocarbons in the vapors worming into her lungs. She coughed and stumbled into the room, her foot catching on a fine trip line that ignited a flame in the far corner of the room.

Oh my God. She was going to burn alive.

The flames began to consume the curtains across the room, their blaze lighting up the entire space so brightly it hurt her eyes. Mya ran to the nearest door as the flames tore across the floor. Locked from the outside? She grabbed a floor lamp and tried to break a window, but there was wood boarded up behind the glass panes. Over and over she slammed the brass fixture into various windows, but whomever had wanted to keep people out had done a damn good job at making sure no one would ever escape from the inside either. She swung around, screaming, the heat surging at her back. She dropped to her knees, coughing in the thick, black smoke.

What would Cole, her firefighter brother, do? She could

try to get upstairs and escape from there, but what if the windows were boarded up there, too? Heat rose and the smoke was thicker in the stairway going up, so that left downstairs. Maybe there was something she could push toward an egress window and climb out of. She crouched over, hurrying back to the basement stairwell. At the stairs, she pulled the door shut behind her, praying that she wasn't sealing her own tomb.

NINETEEN

J ack stood at the airport window gazing out into the pre-dawn inkiness as the plane arrived that would carry him across the globe. He could've slept sitting up as quiet as the airport was, but his bleary eyes refused to shut. His brain unable to get the message that Mya really wasn't going to call and offer him a perfectly reasonable explanation for why she hadn't shown up.

But she'd already made her choice, and it didn't include him. How could he have been so wrong?

He put a forearm against the cool glass, seeing Timber rise from her seat in the window's reflection. She approached him cautiously, but he didn't turn around. They hadn't spoken much since she'd shown up at the departure gate over an hour ago, explaining that Dr. Erickson was arranging their replacements at the University so she'd be joining them a day or two later than expected.

He'd follow up with Lilith upon arrival. He wasn't in any mood to talk to anyone unless she had hazel eyes, sassy dimples, and a body built for his hands. He groaned quietly and leaned his forehead against his arm. His breath fogged the window glass as he tried to erase her from his thoughts.

Impossible.

"Is there anything I can do to help you prepare for our sojourn in Jerusalem?" Timber asked.

He lifted his head, rubbing his eyes. "No, but I appreciate your thoroughness." *Just leave me to my misery.*

He turned around as a commotion erupted down the hall a few gates away. It was all the more pronounced because it had been so silent before. Police began to herd individuals to one side of the building, while three helmeted, gun-bearing SWAT officers spread out in a deliberate fashion toward Jack's gate.

What the hell?

"Timber Hollows, you're under arrest. Put your hands on your head and drop—"

"No!" The graduate student yelled gutturally and lunged for a child sleeping on the opposite bench from her. The scene exploded into action. The center SWAT officer went to his left knee to sight his rifle, while other officers continued to evacuate the area and surround Timber.

Jack moved to the left, watching Timber's grip tighten around the startled toddler's neck. *Jesus Christ.* He turned to the SWAT officer who was trying to round him up with the other bystanders. "She's in my department. Let me try to talk to her."

The officer's eyebrows pulled down lower. "If that baby gets one shade darker blue, it's over."

Jack nodded and turned back to Timber who was now crying almost as much as the toddler's mother. "Timber, *stop.* I don't know why you're doing this, but let the little girl go, and we can talk about it, okay?"

Timber squeezed her eyes shut and shook her head as

the child squirmed wildly. "It's not okay. It's not *ever* going to be okay." Her eyes opened, black makeup tracking down her cheeks. Her gaze cut him deeply, but he didn't understand why.

"You are a woman of logic, Timber. This is neither an expedient nor scientific way to solve your problem. Let me help you."

She shook her head, her lips quivering. "Fuck love. Love isn't logical."

"No, it isn't." Jack desperately wanted her fingers to relax on that child's neck. Behind him, the SWAT officers' tension was a palpable thing. He didn't know how much longer they'd let him attempt to negotiate. "Love can make us damned miserable, but the choice you're contemplating would bring you unhappiness that would far outlast this short-term adrenaline flood you're high on right now. Use your powers of reason, Timber, please. Release the little girl." He held his breath as the fingers of one hand looked like they were relaxing.

"I just wanted to make you happy," she whispered, before clamping her hands roughly against the child's neck, lifting and shaking her violently.

Jack froze as the bullet whistled through the air, slicing into Timber's brain. The grad student collapsed, knees-chest-face to the ground, her head twisted to the side, eyes open and unseeing, a thin red pool spreading out across the commercial-grade carpet.

Jack gasped, roughly shoved aside as law enforcement swooped in to surround Timber and see to the toddler. Jack walked woodenly toward the officer checking Timber's pulse. A cold feeling poured through him. He had a sudden overwhelming need to hold Mya. "What else did Timber do?" he demanded.

"Sit down, Mr. Whiteside. We'll brief you in a few minutes."

"You know my name? What's going on? Do you know anything about Mya Castillo or Lilith Erickson?"

The officer got in his face. "I said, sit down and *stay put*."

Jack didn't sit. He pulled out his cell phone and dialed Mya with shaking fingers. He tried her number twice more when he finally realized someone was calling his name frantically.

Mya? He hurdled over several suitcases and skirted rows of seats until he saw her.

"Mya! My God, what the fuck is going on? Timber's d—Jesus, you're hurt!" Her face was a map of scratches and bruises, her forehead covered with a thick bandage.

And she smelled like a gas can.

He pulled her into his arms and curled his body as tightly as possible around her, knowing without being told that she'd suffered something that would haunt them both for a long time to come. "After waiting for you for more than an hour, I returned to your house and saw that you'd read the note. I thought you'd decided you no longer wanted me."

"I thought you wanted to let me down easy, but I was going to face you anyway. Then Timber had other plans for me."

He pulled back and placed his palms on her cheeks, careful of her cuts. "I can't believe this."

"*Te quería.* She loved you, Jack. She left the note in your truck, saying I held you back from your dreams."

Even as Mya explained the sequence of events, he shook his head, trying to comprehend it. Somehow she had managed to move a workbench in the basement to one of the small, not-to-code egress windows, then used her fist wrapped in a curtain she'd taken from upstairs to smash through the glass. Then she used the curtain to protect herself from the worst of the broken glass to slide through the window. By the time she emerged from the house, sirens were already sounding down the block. Her brother Cole had been on duty, hosing her down in the middle of the street to prevent the gasoline from further damaging her skin until the ambulance arrived to take her to the hospital.

Jack pulled her to him and wouldn't let her go as they answered questions put to them by various law enforcement officers. Afterwards, Jack kissed Mya's hair, angling her toward the hallway. "Let's get you back to the hospital."

Mya stopped him with a hand to his chest. "No."

Contrary to the end. "What do you mean, *no*? We need to make sure the gasoline residue is completely flushed from your skin and hair."

"They've done all they can do. I'll take several more showers in the next twenty four hours, but listen to me."

Her eyes were *so* earnest. He'd never love another woman the way he loved her. He kissed her gently until she pulled back.

"*Listen.* Before anything else gets in the way again." She took a deep breath, her gaze steady and serious. "I'd love to never leave my family, but I want to make a home with you. You *are* my home. Where you are, there I shall be." She pulled a piece of paper from her back pocket and held it up for him.

A plane ticket. To Jerusalem.

His throat tightened. "You just secured a sponsorship for a new studio. And what about Nat and Andre?"

"Cole and Ivy have said before they'd settle into my place if I ever had to move. My place is bigger anyway, and that way Nat and Andre don't have to move all their things."

"What if you lose the sponsorship by the time we get back?" He held his breath, his heart thudding in his chest. He had to make sure she'd thought this through.

That she wanted him as much as he needed her.

As soon as he saw her racing toward him moments ago, he knew he'd never be able to walk away from her again. Knew he was done with long-term assignments overseas.

He held back a smile as she put on a determined face.

"My sponsor told me tonight that he'd planned to help me start a new studio whether we placed in the top three or not. He really believes in my mission. What we've started brainstorming is bigger than either of us imagined. It'll take a long time to implement all our plans. He and I can stay in touch and plan everything online. And if he has a problem with me being gone..." she shrugged, "well, then it wasn't meant to be. I'll move to plan B. I refuse to miss any more time with you."

He laced their fingers together, moved by how much she was willing to sacrifice for him. She had only her purse and her phone, yet she was ready to walk into the unknown with him all the way to the other side of the world. He kissed her knuckles and looked in her eyes. "Mya, I've loved you ever since you rode your hot pink bicycle over my cousin Blake when he broke my Geode Growing Kit. We've matured, together and individually, creating layers like the earth. Those stratifications tell a story. Ours will be fascinating to mine when we're old and gray." He kissed her lips.

She laid her palm over his chest. "What are you saying?"

"When I asked you to come to Horsetooth, I'd planned

to tell you I want to start over with you here in Fort Collins. I want to teach and get married and start a family."

"Really?" Moisture welled in her eyes making them sparkle.

"I've never been more sure of anything."

TWENTY

3 *weeks later*

MYA SAT on top of the picnic table in the middle of her backyard, surrounded by all the people she loved most in the world, swiping at the tears that wouldn't abate tonight. *Happy tears.* Cole, her brave brother who'd carried the weight of their family on his broad shoulders when their *papi* died and their mother got so sick...he was finally being rewarded for his long years of selflessness.

He'd just gotten down on one knee and proposed to the love of his life, Ivy.

Of course, she'd said yes.

Mya had helped her brother set it all up. The night, the food, the music from the mariachi band...the people...It was all magical, as if they'd special-ordered the night just so. The stars had begun to pulse, piercing the gauzy haze of the falling dusk above the dozen strings of white lights that Mya had spent all afternoon arranging between the silent, stately cottonwood trees that communed between Rosie's and her backyard. Crickets, happy that August had finally come, chirped, calling to their own, their song a pleasant harmony to the buzz of voices flooding the yards with congratulations, jokes, and speculation about how many people would have to be seated in overflow for the upcoming wedding.

Cole slid onto the picnic table beside her, then bumped her shoulder with his own like he'd always done when she was a moody teen who thought she didn't need anyone. Not her dead and buried father. Her sick mother. Certainly not a big brother who stuck his damn nose in her business Every. Single. Day.

Time and perspective had given her new eyes.

This time she bumped him back and wiped her eyes on his sleeve. She looked over and caught his grin.

"Getting emotional in your old age, I see," he said, eyes twinkling like their father's had.

She sniffled harder, her lips beginning to wobble. "Don't you d-dare make me get the ugly c-cries in front of this crowd, or I'll make sure you regret it, *hermano*."

He nodded earnestly. "I don't doubt it for a second." His lips curled up once more as he slung an arm around her shoulders. "Thanks again for all your help today...and for everything you've done to help with Nat and Andre over the last couple of years. I'm really proud of you, *lobita*."

Little wolf. His name for her since she'd been a child. She couldn't speak right now so she turned her head into the nook of his shoulder and squeezed him around the waist.

Cole patted her back. "Hey, *heeey. Es una noche maravillosa, no?* Let's have you dry those tears...especially if you don't want me to make up some story about your period to the guy who's headed our way with a look on his face like he's ready to mount his white horse and ride on up to the castle to slay his lady's dragon. That dragon being me."

Mya peeked her head up from Cole's embrace to see Jack striding across the yard, his long legs eating up the space, his white shirt sleeves rolled up to expose strong forearms, his face set in serious lines. Here was a man on a mission, his eyes behind those sexy glasses laser-focused on her, seemingly oblivious to anything and everything he passed—the band crooning to Rosie as she blushed, children laughing and running, high on sugar and the energy of the night, couples dancing under lights that softly swayed in the gentle, late summer breeze coming off the foothills. He bypassed it all, his face a study of concentration, and for Mya, everything fell away.

Cole kissed her cheek and slipped away. In the next heartbeat, Jack held out his hand for her, and she took it without a word. He drew her into his arms and kissed her long and slow and deep like there weren't fifty of their closest friends and family milling around them. Kissed her like his life depended on it. Kissed her so she was weak and breathless and completely undone when he finally lifted his head and smiled into her eyes like all was now truly right in the world.

Raucous applause and whistles rang through the night around them, the mariachi band shifting their attention to them. Captive to the band, Jack kept her plastered to his side, his hand wandering so incessantly her cheeks heated until she decided to distract him with a dance. When their bodies began moving to the music, the musicians shifted their next song to a slower, heart-throbbing tune. This night would ever be etched in her memory.

They danced for hours, and when the last of the guests

filtered to their cars or taxis, laughing and reinforced with hope for the vagaries and troubles of life, Mya and Jack linked hands and went in search of Rosie. They found her fast asleep in Mya's bed. Jack closed the door softly, then chuckled, the deep sound making Mya's heart alert and eager.

"You realize she planned it this way," he said, drawing her back out into the night, walking with her under the strings of lights to Rosie's place.

"So we'd have her place to ourselves tonight. I love her so much, for so many reasons." Mya tipped her head back and breathed deep.

"You want to stay out here longer?" He suppressed a yawn.

She looked at him, smiling, knowing everything she was feeling was out there, raw and open in her gaze. "I only want to be where you are."

He made a distinctively masculine noise in his throat and grabbed her, wrapping her around his trunk as was their way, and entered the house where he took her straight to the bedroom, not bothering with the lights. Tenderly, he lowered her back on the blankets, then stepped away to open the curtains to let the light of their happy backyards spill across the bed.

She went up on her knees to pull the covers back, then stripped her strappy sundress off. Clad in nothing but her silky fuchsia underwear, she watched his clever fingers unbuttoning his shirt with deliberation. One button at a time, his chest came into view, then his abs, and she felt her body go liquid. She shivered in anticipation.

"Are you cold?" he asked, his voice low, his eyes like a predator, raking over her nakedness.

"Not one bit. In fact, I feel slightly feverish. I think I need a doctor."

He wrapped a palm—warm, big, gentle—around her neck, guiding her back into the pillows. "I'm a different kind of doctor, my love, but I *know* I can fix what's ailing you."

Ooo, such confidence. "Show me."

"Always so demanding." His body covered her, and they both moaned at the long-awaited contact. She wriggled her legs, anxious to feel him settle into the cradle of her pelvis. He lifted his weight slightly so she could spread her thighs.

"I love you," she whispered. She felt him at her center, hot, throbbing, perfect. "For always, Jack. This time I'm not letting you go. I hope you know what you're getting into with me and my family."

"You should know by now I like layers. I'll never let you push me away again. You are mine, and I am yours."

She gasped as he filled her slowly, his gaze locked on hers.

"You are mine, and I am yours," she repeated.

Waves of desire built and crashed over them as the first fingers of dawn crept over the mountains in their backyard, and he showed her just how much he'd always love her.

And she finally believed.

DEAR READER,

Thank you for spending time with Jack and Mya! If you enjoyed their story, please consider leaving a review on your retailer of choice. After buying books, it's the next best way you can support your favorite authors.

And now...if you like pulse-pounding romantic suspense, read on for a sneak peek at a love story about a blue-jeans wearing CEO and a boutique owner with dangerous secrets to keep...

Hugs & happy ever afters,
Misty
xoxo

And now, Zack and Sloane's story...

"A heroine to root for, a hero to die for, Misty Dietz has crafted a classic romantic suspense in the tradition of Kay Hooper. A winning debut!"

~ Allison Brennan, NYT Bestselling Author

CHAPTER 1

Zack Goldman slapped at a mosquito and leaned against his truck as Morgan Sawyer sashayed down his rutted gravel driveway like she'd driven up in a limo instead of a Corolla sporting a spare tire. She was the sister he'd never had, earning her PhD in urban wiles and tomfoolery when they were adolescents—alone, but not so innocent—on the streets.

He'd bet his river-side acreage that she'd left the cryptic *WHERE IS SHE* note on his door this morning to punk him. Something was definitely going on if she was up this early. Especially on a Sunday. "I was on my way into town. After my errands, I was going to stop by your place to see if you were still alive. Haven't seen you in weeks. How'd you manage to crawl out of bed before noon?"

Her red-painted lips tilted up at the corners. "Haven't gone to bed yet."

He pushed away from the truck and ruffled her pixie-short blonde hair. "*Brat.* You come all the way out here to spy on me, or are you finally going to ask me for a job?"

She shook her head. "You're too boring to spy on nowadays. But damn, I'd pay good money to watch you roll somebody over a pool table again."

"Those days are long gone, Morgan."

"Never say never."

The way she said it made Zack's shoulders tense. *I should have brought you to Sunday suppers with John more often.* A mistake he'd never be able to fix since John, his plain-speaking, charismatic mentor—the only person he'd ever strived to emulate—had been buried for almost a year now.

Zack battened down the lid of his grief. "Nice try with the mysterious note you left on my door. You should know by now I don't bring women out here." Didn't bring *anyone*. He appreciated his five acres of elbow room.

Morgan's eyebrows rose. "What note?"

A cold sensation rippled through him. She looked too intrigued to be lying. "Never mind." His thoughts raced. If Morgan hadn't left the note, who had? And why? It had to be either a mistake, or a joke. His inner circle was two men and three women. Five people who didn't share his blood but were the only family he'd ever known. The only ones who'd never betrayed him.

His mentor, John Samuels, was dead. Morgan was here. Twyla and Archie Raessler were at home as of fifteen minutes ago when Archie had texted him...

The only one not accounted for was John's daughter, Ann. She hadn't answered his phone call a half hour ago when he'd first found the note. Zack's pulse throbbed in his neck.

Don't miss the sun today by worrying about the rain coming tomorrow. One of John's positive affirmations.

Maybe Ann had finally taken his advice and unglued her phone from her hand.

Time to get on with the day. "What do you need, Morgan, I should get going."

"Can't I simply come to visit?"

He crossed his arms. "At six-thirty on a Sunday morning?"

"Maybe I'm turning over a new leaf." When he smirked, she sighed. "*Fine.* I want to have a shindig for Ann out here in the boonies. When she's ready to share the news, that is. We'll have a bonfire, drinks, and cookies in the shape of baby bottles. Isn't that the cutest thing you've ever heard? They make them at the deli on 32nd."

He'd derailed about a mile back. "Baby bottles?" Her expression indicated he was a member of the forty watt club, but he still couldn't wrap his mind around baby bottle cookies. "Why would you—"

No.

Morgan cringed. "Oh, damn. How can you *not* know?"

His throat dried. "Stop bullshitting, brat. If Ann's pregnant, so am I."

"Well, in that case, we'll get more cookies."

Her grin fueled his alarm. He drummed his fingers on top of his head, but that didn't help, so he cussed. A lot.

"Sorry, big guy. Guess she knew you'd react this way so she was obviously waiting to tell you. She'll probably thank me for breaking it to you, now that I think about it. But yeah, she got knocked up."

Morgan's voice faded into the background while questions ran circles in his mind. *Who? When?* He was ready to throttle Ann for not telling him right away. But first, maybe he'd better throw himself under a bus. Not fifteen minutes ago he was wondering if she had a boyfriend so he could do a background check on the guy, and now he finds out she's having a *baby?*

She's just a kid herself.

No way. "All right, joke's on me. Give it up, Morgan." She was probably lying about the WHERE IS SHE note, too.

Her dimples deepened. "Better get your mad out before you see her."

"I'm *not* mad." Really, he wasn't. Just shocked. And guilty. John had made him promise to look out for Ann when he was dust because she had no one else. His pulse pounded in his neck. *John's grandchild.* "How is it she told you before me?"

Morgan's face went blank for a second. "She didn't exactly tell me. I kinda guessed with her feeling sick so much lately."

Oh, that. He'd chalked it up to the stress of her recent move and the coming anniversary of John's death. But then, he hadn't asked, had he?

What were they going to do with a *baby*? He was acting like a stereotypical idiot bachelor, but *damn*. What if the sperm donor wasn't there for her? He couldn't let Ann's kid grow up without a father figure. John hadn't come into his life until he was an adult and look how messed up *his* adolescence had been.

He checked the time on his phone. *Six-forty-one.* He tried Ann's home and cell numbers again, leaving messages when voicemail picked up. Then he slipped the phone into his pocket. "Who is it?"

Morgan had been squinting across the river. Her gaze scooted back to him. "Who?"

"The boogey man. Who else, Morgan? The *father.*"

She shrugged. "No idea. Sure is a secretive little bug, huh?"

He frowned at her grin, and his gut cartwheeled. "I'll get back to you on that party thing, okay?"

"No sweat, big guy."

He heard her laugh as he slid into his truck and gunned it down the gravel driveway.

The only thing he hated worse than a coward was a deserter. And deserter dads topped the list. Somebody's head was gonna roll.

CHAPTER 2

Zack had his blood pressure under control by the time he pulled up to the service entrance of Skinny Dipping, a frou frou home furnishings boutique where Ann had recently scored the part-time job of her dreams. Or so she'd claimed. He hadn't been here yet, but he'd been curious about it, not only because Ann talked it up, but also because a moniker like that conjured good mojo.

He cut the engine and stepped into the spill of sunshine, industrial sounds from the front of the mall reassuring him that his construction crew was still on the job. On a Sunday. Early. Hopefully wrapping things up because the amusement park addition was scheduled to open in two days. Two more days of burning the candle on both ends, and he'd give all his crew fat bonuses.

Skinny Dipping's plain steel door looked no different from any of the others along the back of the mall, except this one was propped open. He knocked and peered inside. Finding no one, he zigzagged through stacks of boxes toward a door that presumably led to the showroom.

While the back room blazed with ugly fluorescent lighting, the store itself was like the backdrop for a chick flick, glowing with strategically placed lamps, wall lanterns, and lights that dripped crystals.

Getting no response to repeated calls, he continued deeper into the store. Silly, sparkling things—paperweights? —sat on fat wooden candlesticks any self-respecting Boy Scout could carve. He kept his hands in his pockets as he carefully bypassed chunky necklaces draped over stilettos, fuzzy blankets that wouldn't keep anyone warm, tiny pots that reeked, painted and beat-up furniture, smelly candles, and a ridiculous assortment of gaudy accessories. Honest to God, the sensory smorgasbord made him lightheaded.

This place is an epic fire hazard.

Ann's motive for working here *had* to be educational since she didn't need the money. She wanted to enroll in NDSU's interior design program but was conflicted about walking away from her father's construction business. Zack had told her she could do both, but so far she hadn't made any moves.

Though with a baby coming, who knew when that would happen—*or if.*

He frowned, reaching for a flimsy blue scarf on impulse. He ran his fingers down the sheer length, turned a corner, and almost collided with a pair of legs on a ladder.

His eyes traveled from the three-inch heeled sandals with ribbons that wound up delicate ankles, inch by satiny inch, until—*Jesus*—what had to be almost three and a half feet later his eyes feasted on an ass in white denim.

"Hey there, be with you in a sec." Her voice was like caramel. The kind you suck on. And her scent, warm vanilla. He twisted the scarf between his fists. *Say something.* The woman went up on her toes to arrange a feather boa on a shelf and damned if those Daisy Dukes didn't raise several tantalizing centimeters, exposing the generous swell of her buttocks.

And no tan line. He stifled a groan.

She started down the ladder, and he rubbed a hand over his heart and backed up. He hadn't had such a visceral response to a woman since...*ever?*

"Thanks for waiting. You here for the daybed pickup?" she asked.

"Yeah. *No!* Ah, sorry. That's not why I'm here." *Tongue-tied even?* The woman stood with one brow raised, arms crossed under her small breasts, the billowy-type shirt doing nothing to conceal the flare of her hips.

Hips just begging for...

He shut his eyes on a slow blink, forcing himself to focus on his purpose. His face heated before he set the scarf on a table and extended his hand. "I'm Zack Goldman. I work with Ann at Samuel's Construction."

The woman looked at his hand, hesitating. Yeah, his hands were rough, but they were clean. Maybe she was a germophobe or something.

A second later, though, she placed her hand in his, and the jolt must have been mutual. Her eyes widened. Weren't they an unusual gray-brown? The color he'd imagine on a she-wolf.

Purpose. Ann. Baby. "The back door was open. Ann told me she'd be here early one of these mornings to help out, but I couldn't remember when," he said.

"Ann was scheduled to be here by six to help with yesterday's freight, but she hasn't arrived yet. Have you tried her at home? I figured she'd slept in. I'm Sloane Swift, by the way."

Flamboyant clothing and enough noisy arm bangles to accessorize a band of gypsies... Her name matched the package. Large, darkly-lashed eyes anchored an oval face above cheekbones sculpted by a master. And all that soft, smooth skin...

Was frowning.

He looked down at their joined hands, let go, and shoved his own in his pockets. "Ann's not answering her phone."

Sloane was about to say something when a tiny blonde whizzed around the corner. "Hey, boss." The woman's eyes moved from Sloane to Zack, her smile warming a hundred degrees. "Hey handsome, don't let me chase you away. I'm Tori Daily—the manager."

"Zack Goldman. I work with Ann."

A brief disturbance crossed her features before she pinned the smile back in place. "So *you're* Zack. Ann told me you're donating a kidney to a friend's wife. When are you doing that?"

Sloane raised her eyebrows, and his face warmed again. "They hope to do the transplant shortly after Twyla has the baby. Anyway—"

"I hadn't heard the woman was pregnant. That's cool. I'm sure Ann will keep us posted." Tori turned back to Sloane. "Where is she anyway? She was pumped to see the new stuff."

"She's not here yet." Sloane gazed steadily at Zack.

Don't be afraid of women with balls or brains. You don't want no box of rocks. John had been down on his knees trowling concrete with Zack's crew of eight when he'd shared that bit of counsel so long ago.

Zack shifted his weight, then realized how weak that made him look. He could really do without all the unbidden Johnisms today.

"That's not like her. She sick?" Tori asked.

Ann was usually conscientious to a fault. So where was she? That cryptic note was making him more bent by the minute. "I'm sure there's a reasonable excuse."

"Yeah, you're probably right." Tori studied her nails.

She's lying.

Either she knew where Ann was, or she sucked at reassuring people. Maybe both. Zack's phone chirped to signal an incoming text from his CFO. *Benji's irate. Better be here in 20 or better.*

Now what? Once he was done with Timothy

Benjamin's mall amusement park and the sub-contractors were paid, he was never going to work with a scumbag like him again. He frowned at Sloane. "Sorry for the trouble. I'm sure Ann will feel terrible about being late."

"We'll be fine. But maybe you should stop by her place to check on her? She could be ill or something."

It was the *or something* he didn't care to think about. But since he needed to deal with Benjamin, and the Samuel's office wasn't far from Ann's, he might as well stop over there. "Yeah, I'll drop by her place in an hour or so."

"Be sure to have her call us so we know everything's okay. And hey, the transplant thing's pretty neat." Sloane's eyes smiled, making something warm pass through his chest. He nodded and made his way outside, itching to run for miles. He couldn't decide who frustrated him more— Benjamin for making his crew hate their jobs, himself for being in the dark about Ann's mystery man and his gut-level response to Sloane, and John, for making him care about it all in the first place.

CHAPTER 3

Sloane continued to look at the back door for several moments after Zack's departure, not sure what to think. Tori wrestled a box off a dolly and drew a box cutter across the packing tape. "Quite the eye candy, eh?"

Sloane rubbed her hands on her forearms. "Silky black hair, stormy green eyes, and five o'clock shadow. Tall, built, and moody. In a word? Yummy."

Tori smirked. "Yeah, he seems like the whole package. Besides being gorgeous and obviously altruistic, he's successful. Samuel's Construction is one of the largest contractors in the upper Midwest. Ann's father could have had any number of front runners take over the business, but Zack's been the man running the show these last few years even before John died. Weird thing is, Ann says women fawn all over him, but he doesn't even seem to notice. I bet he's gay."

"He's not gay."

"I have several male friends who you'd never think—"

"So do I. The hetero vibe was in full force, Tori. Your loss if you missed it."

Tori paused in the act of lifting an ivory reproduction of *Nymph and Satyr Carousing*. "We've been friends for fifteen years, and I've never seen you so instantly gaga over a guy." She pointed the carved model at Sloane. "I'd hate to see you disappointed if he's not in your market."

Sloane eased the satyr out of her manager's grasp. *Definitely time to change the topic.* "Speaking of men, when will Teddy be in town? You guys have been dating for a month now, and I still haven't met him. You're making him up, aren't you?"

She relaxed when Tori took the bait and launched into a diatribe about her busy, out of town boyfriend. Sloane set *Nymph and Satyr* on a velvet-covered pedestal and drifted from box to box, unloading freight, barely noticing the beautiful objects that normally gave her so much pleasure.

Truth was, she was unnerved by her response to Zack Goldman. Sure, the man was a looker and—wow, obviously unselfish—but even more than that...

He'd sent her energy. And she hadn't even touched anything metallic. Her nerve endings were still sparking like they were having an orgy. That unexpected encounter of his energy was all...*beach heat, rolling waves, and oil-slicked bodies sliding together in a dim cabana.*

It had felt delicious.

Carnal.

That unsettled her more than anything.

She couldn't remember the last time she'd physically touched someone who didn't require her to envision her energy shield—that unfortunate but necessary layer of protection that prevented people from short-circuiting her equanimity. No one could see it, but Lordy, she could feel it. Especially if she was too late to initiate her shield.

So what the heck had happened with Zack? That encounter left her...*hungry.* And wasn't that interesting?

Crap. What was she thinking? He was one apple she wasn't biting. If he'd instigated that kind of reaction in her, she couldn't—*wouldn't*—do that to him. Anyone who glided that effortlessly through her barriers always ended up burned. Her gift was largely uncontrollable.

A curse.

And a source of danger to anyone who got too close.

The cascading trickle of water in the fountain broke her reflection, and she looked up to find herself snared in one of

Tori's scowls. The *I know there's something going on and I'm going to hound you until it's on the table* kind of stare that had Sloane's heart revving. Tori was one of a handful of people who knew about her object reading burden—that whacked liability her mother referred to as a "gift."

Unlike shielding herself from people's energies, which she struggled to manage, Sloane had become quite masterful at silencing this other ability. But because Tori knew what she was capable of—touching metallic objects to infer information about their history via latent energy fields —Sloane let her guard down more easily around her. Except for times like now when it made her feel...over-exposed. Because, wow, it was really creepy when you thought about it.

She forced a smile and moved to arrange a pile of pillows to give her hands something to do. "When Teddy's back in town, I'll have you guys over for supper."

Tori pursed her lips. "Knock it off. I saw you shake Zack's hand. You read something when you touched him, didn't you?"

"You know I don't like it when you bring that up."

Tori leaned forward. "I *knew* it."

Sloane's hands started to sweat. She wanted away. From this conversation. From this despicable affliction that required so much effort to ignore. She marched through the storeroom and out the back door. The August air clung heavy and damp to her skin. Did this classify as pouting?

Lord, she hated pouters.

"Sloane?"

She turned to find Tori's head peeking around the steel door.

"Your lip's dragging. Pick it up and—" Tori burst into laughter. Sloane looked back at the parking lot to see her part-time employee Carmen Miller sauntering up in a straining-at-the-seams leopard print dress, wheeling an enormous purple suitcase.

"*Whew*. So hot out here I nearly left my ass on the leather car seat. Shake a leg, girlies. I wanna see the loot."

Sloane closed her eyes, breathed deep, and concentrated on the beat of her heart, using the rhythm to summon the energy required to raise her protection shield before she put an arm around Tori to follow the wide-hipped redhead inside. Carmen leaned the suitcase against the wall, grabbed a handful of Kleenexes, and stuffed them into her pillowy cleavage before opening the staff refrigerator.

Sloane gestured to the luggage. "Mind me asking what you plan to do with the mobile unit, Carm?"

Carmen rubbed a pop can against her cheek. "I'm facing reality. No way am I gonna be able to pass up a lot of this new stuff. And I don't trust Miss Salad Shooter over there to not poach my digs until I can get it all home. Hence, the carry-on."

"*Carry-on?* More like semi-truck trailer. And a fugly one at that." Tori wrinkled her nose at the beat up baggage.

"You're just sorry you didn't think of it yourself, short stuff. So where's Annie? Bet that twit's already on the floor, huh? She was happy as a hooker on sailor's payday to see what was comin' in."

Sloane took a water bottle from the fridge. "She isn't here yet. She's not answering her cell or home numbers either."

"Really? I busted my rump to get here early so she wouldn't get all the good stuff first. That girl likes to shop more than I do. I hope her big doin' last night went alright."

Sloane frowned. "What was she going to do?"

"Wouldn't say. She blushed pinker than a sunburned tittie, though, which means it had to be about a *man*."

Tori began to pace. "I don't like this."

Sloane didn't either. "Oh, stop it. I'm sure she's fine. You girls head out onto the floor and get as much unloaded as you can. I'll help as soon as I have this paperwork in order. I want the store to look less like a war zone by the time Mr. Benjamin stops in later."

Sloane plopped into her desk chair, tucked a lock of hair behind her ear, and reached for a clipboard. "Oh, and Tori? Speaking of Mr. Benjamin, can you pull the new numbered Swarovski rhino? He wants to add it to his collection, which is excellent, since he has all but committed to sponsoring Project Broken Wings. Anything at the store he wants, he gets. Okay?"

Not getting a response, she set the clipboard down and swiveled in her seat to find her manager staring at her. "Tori?"

"Oh, God."

Sloane's neck tingled. "Something happen to the rhino?"

"I, Ann, we... Ah, *crap*. Ann wanted to see how the crystal would look in her curio when it was all lit up. So, I told her you wouldn't mind if she took it out on loan, to see if it would fit in with her...other...pretty things." Tori twisted her fingers in her skirt. "But, you do mind, don't you?"

Sloane tried not to panic. Really, it wasn't a big deal. Or it wouldn't be, if so much wasn't riding on maintaining a relationship with Timothy Benjamin. She'd have to start looking for sponsors all over again if he wouldn't sponsor Project Broken Wings—the suicide support alliance that she'd dreamt of founding since her sister Megan's tragic death.

She rubbed a hand on her stomach. "So you're sure Ann has it at home?"

"Yes. I'm sorry, Sloane. I didn't know Benjamin wanted it."

"No, of course you didn't." Sloane chewed on her lip and looked at her watch. It wasn't even eight o'clock yet. Benjamin most likely wouldn't be here before the store opened at noon. Then again, it wouldn't be out of character for him to come earlier and demand a private showing.

Tori plucked at her skirt. "Call Ann. Even if she's not home, Zack said he was going to stop at her place in about an hour. By the time you grab a latte, he'll probably be there. Ann told me he has a key. You could ask to go in and have a look around."

"I'll call, but how about you go?" *Please.*

"I can't, two college summer school students are interviewing me for a class project at nine."

Dang. "Right. Okay, would you ask Carmen to go?" Sloane mentally crossed her fingers, toes, and any other body parts that were crossable.

"Naw. She hasn't seen the crystal yet. Why does it matter who goe— Oh. *Zack.*"

"Zip it. There's no 'oh, Zack.'" Sloane pretended to dig into her paperwork. After a few long seconds, Tori slipped out the door, and Sloane picked up the phone.

Four minutes later, she sat with her head in her hands. Ann still wasn't answering either number.

The day was rapidly deteriorating. Her choices? Face the beefcake who made her body remember she was a freak, or show up empty-handed to the man with the money and connections to make her dream come true. A dream that could help heal so many other families affected by suicide.

A dream that straddled the fence with a secret that would never release her.

A secret Tori didn't even know.

It had taken two years to get a bite from a sponsor. She *had* to stay in good graces with Benjamin. He would deny her the money to start her foundation if she couldn't produce the rhino. It was exactly the sort of control game he enjoyed. So she'd either have to get used to crap like that, or start all over.

Her legs felt wobbly as she stood. She grabbed her purse and walked to the back door, praying for a low-consequence encounter with Zack. And knowing somehow it wouldn't be.

Ready to read on?
Find Come Hell or High Desire on your preferred retailer now.

And thank you for your support!

ABOUT MISTY DIETZ

*"Dietz brings us a fresh, interesting plot and draws readers
into the entertaining story right from the start."*
~ RT Book Reviews

Misty loves her man, her kids, kayaking, and Dean
Winchester (oh yeah, Supernatural fans unite!). She writes
paranormal, suspense, and contemporary romance, but she
reads anything she can get her hands on, usually with her
fur baby on her lap.

She spends her days writing sexy, adrenaline-fueled
stories, enjoying family and friends, and praying her
children don't come home with math homework. :)

*Misty's social media links...because she would LURRRV to hear
from you!*

www.mistydietz.com
misty@mistydietz.com